"You look [partially covered by barcode sticker] gazin

"You have that glow people talk about."

"I do?" Her cheeks grew warm. Was she still attractive to David after all?

"You look the same way you did when you were expecting Brian. Remember? I used to tease you about it. I said, 'If we could bottle that kind of beauty, we'd make a million dollars.'"

"Yes, I do remember," she said softly. "I always thought you were just trying to make me feel better."

"No, I was dead serious." Slowly, tentatively, David moved from his recliner to the sofa. He took her hand in his, his very nearness making her weak, turning her heart to gelatin. "Rachel, sweetheart, I've been so worried about you. It's Christmas and I hate this animosity between us. Isn't there something we can do to resolve this?"

Tears gathered behind Rachel's eyes. She yearned to feel herself enfolded in his embrace and to pretend that these bitter weeks apart had never happened, that this was like every Christmas they had spent together and would spend together, for the rest of their lives.

"Oh, David." She sighed. No other words would come.

Then he moved toward her and gathered her into his arms....

Books by Carole Gift Page

Love Inspired

In Search of Her Own #4
Decidedly Married #22
Rachel's Hope #40

CAROLE GIFT PAGE

writes from the heart about contemporary issues facing adults. Considered one of America's best-loved Christian fiction writers, Carole was born and raised in Jackson, Michigan. She is the recipient of two Pacesetter Awards and the C.S. Lewis Honor Book Award. Over eight hundred of Carole's stories, articles and poems have been published in more than one hundred Christian periodicals.

A frequent speaker at conferences, schools, churches and women's ministries around the country, Carole finds fulfillment in being able to share her testimony about the faithfulness of God in her life and the abundance He offers those who come to Him. Carole and her husband, Bill, have three children and live in Moreno Valley, California.

Rachel's Hope

Carole Gift Page

Published by Steeple Hill Books™

STEEPLE HILL BOOKS

ISBN 0-373-87040-X

RACHEL'S HOPE

This edition published by arrangement with Steeple Hill Books.

Printed in U.S.A.

Therefore my heart is glad, and my glory rejoiceth:
my flesh also shall rest in hope.

—*Psalm* 16:9

With all my love,
To my mother and father,
Aldon and Millie Gift,
who have loved each other
through over 56 years of marriage.

Chapter One

Rachel Webber stared at the sign over the physician's door, her heart jackhammering and a sour taste at the back of her throat. This moment wasn't real. It had to be a dream. A nightmare.

"This must be it," said Marlene, her throaty, no-nonsense voice sounding distant, disconnected. "It says Dr. Bernard Oberg."

Rachel looked around. She had nearly forgotten Marlene. For one desperate moment she wished their roles were reversed, that Marlene Benson was the expectant mother and Rachel the comforting friend.

"We can't just stand here, Rachel. You want to know for sure, don't you?"

Rachel nodded and reached for the doorknob. As impossible as it seemed, she was actually here, forcing herself to face the truth, however unwelcome it might be. She straightened her shoulders and entered the obstetrician's office, Marlene on her heels. She knew they made a comical spectacle, Marlene nearly shoving her toward the receptionist's desk. She prayed all eyes wouldn't be on her, reading her face, guessing her thoughts. As hard as she struggled to put on a brave front, she was on the verge of tears. She could have been facing a firing squad instead of a mere pregnancy test.

Once inside, Marlene heaved herself into an empty chair, but Rachel paused stonily and gazed past the anonymous faces, wondering if she looked as conspicuous as she felt. But why should she feel so ill at ease? She was an ordinary woman in her early thirties, not unlike the other women in this office. She had as much right to be here as anyone.

Already she was feeling a twinge of claustrophobia mingled with a ripple of nausea. Dr. Oberg's waiting room was too close, too warm. It was an oversize walk-in closet camouflaged with nursery bric-a-brac and semigloss paint. The room was uncomfortably small and narrow, with baby blue walls, bare except for an occasional pastel drawing of a child hugging a pink blanket or clutching a teddy bear. The drawings were signed simply Muriel, with no last name.

"May I help you, ma'am?" asked the woman at the reception desk.

"She means you, Rachel," whispered Marlene. "I don't need this kind of help—thank goodness!"

"This isn't something I bargained for, either," Rachel retorted. She approached the desk and wondered what difference it all made—the walls, the paintings and good old Muriel, whoever she was. There were too many other matters to occupy Rachel's mind. Questions buzzed inside her skull like swarming, relentless bees, unnerving her, nearly incapacitating her. For all too long she had fretted over the possibility of being pregnant—for days, weeks now. As each day had passed, the idea had grown stronger, more pressing, more probable than before. In desperation she had gone to the drugstore and purchased several home pregnancy tests, but each time the positive sign had appeared she'd convinced herself it couldn't be accurate.

Realizing at last that she could no longer keep her anxieties to herself, she had turned to Marlene with her apprehensions. "I can't be pregnant," she had lamented. "David would be absolutely furious."

Always the irrepressible and unflappable ally, Marlene had trumpeted, "And he'd have no one but himself to thank, now, would he!" With that, Marlene had gone to the telephone directory and selected a number—the number of a Long Beach obstetrician, a random choice—and dialed. "Rachel," she'd said, cupping the mouthpiece, "I got you a spot for October 15, at four o'clock." When Rachel had offered a feeble protest, Marlene had simply handed her the phone and said, "It's settled. Here, give her your vital statistics."

But now, standing in this cramped waiting room, Rachel wanted more than anything in the world to turn and run out the door. No, she was through running. She had dodged this dilemma long enough.

"I'm Mrs. Webber...Rachel Webber," she announced to the receptionist-nurse. Why did she sound so infuriatingly apologetic? Unconsciously, she clutched the side of her knit A-line skirt, straightening it, while the young woman in white offered a professional smile. She was rather pretty, Rachel noted impassively, with her blond hair swept back in a meticulous, efficient coronet at the back of her head. She had the kind of controlled, understated beauty one expected of a nurse.

"Yes, Mrs. Webber," the woman replied crisply. "We'll want a urine specimen—you can go right through that door—and when you get back I have some forms for you to fill out."

Rachel lowered her eyes and obediently left the room, her face flushed with warmth. When she returned, she said quietly, "I left the specimen in the bathroom."

"Fine. Now, why don't you have a seat and fill out these forms?"

"How long will it take? I mean, I can find out right away, right? It's not like you have to wait and see if the rabbit dies or anything."

Again the receptionist flashed her polite, detached smile. "Yes, Mrs. Webber, we'll have the results promptly. If you'll just take a seat, the doctor will see you in about half an hour."

"Thank you." Rachel slipped into a vacant chair beside Marlene and tried her best to look nonchalant as she forced a placid expression into place. But her cheeks felt hot, her lips stiff and tight against her teeth. Her face—a mask of aloof indifference—felt so brittle she had the sensation it might shatter if she let down her guard and allowed her surging emotions to break through the protective veneer.

Thank goodness Marlene was there with her. She didn't have to face this thing alone. She knew she and Marlene made an unlikely duo—Rachel a young housewife and Marlene a middle-aged widow. Marlene was ten years older than Rachel and looked older still. She wore no makeup and kept her dark brown hair in a loose bun at the nape of her neck. Marlene was large boned and, as she laughingly described herself, a bit broad in the beam. "Just call me a big roly-poly teddy bear," she would say with a note of self-deprecation. She often complained that no matter where she shopped, she could never find clothing that fit properly. "I'm waiting for tents to come back in style," she would tell a perplexed salesgirl. Then with a raucous laugh she'd add, "Not tent dresses...army surplus tents!"

That's what I may be needing soon! Rachel thought darkly.

"Relax," Marlene soothed. "It's not the end of the world."

"Maybe not, but I think I can see it from here," Rachel said dryly. She set her purse at her feet and leaned back, crossing her legs at the ankle. Marlene's right, she told herself. This isn't the end of the world. She gazed ahead at nothing in particular, at the pastel child in the painting clutching his teddy bear, at the blue wall. She breathed deeply, willing her taut muscles to unwind.

Lately, she reflected somberly, it was impossible to relax. She couldn't read through an entire article in a magazine. She couldn't even concentrate on the paperback she'd brought along in her purse. How could she possibly relax when she might be going home to David with a positive pregnancy test?

She could not afford to be pregnant now. A pregnancy would change her whole life; it would ruin everything. She didn't want to know, but soon she would know. In a half hour a doctor she had never seen before would come and tell her the future course of her life—just like that, the whole future course. How ironic could you get?

Marlene was chuckling over a *Baby Time* magazine, scanning pages of adorable, bouncing babies and shaking her head. "Deliver me!" she said.

And me along with you, thought Rachel.

For the first time since entering the waiting room, she dared to let her gaze focus on the other clients. A young couple, surely just teenagers, sat close to each other on an orange vinyl couch. The girl, in a flannel shirt and bib overalls, flipped idly through a baby magazine. The boy, tall and lanky with stringy, shoulder-length brown hair, studied the walls and ceiling with an intense concentration while tapping knobby fingers nervously on the arm of the couch.

"Look at this beautiful nursery furniture, Jeff," Rachel heard the girl say. "Whitewashed oak! Wouldn't you love to have that for the baby?"

The boy glanced at the picture, grunted and stared back at the ceiling. "Your mother doesn't have room in her house for that kind of stuff," he answered hoarsely. "We'll be lucky to squeeze in a crib."

"Poor kids," Marlene murmured from behind her magazine.

Another woman, dark haired and plain—perhaps in her early thirties, like Rachel—sat serenely reading a book. Rachel couldn't help staring. The woman was huge, monstrous. She was obviously due any moment now. Had Rachel been that large when she carried Brian? She couldn't have been, but she couldn't remember. It had been thirteen years ago.

The woman looked up, catching Rachel's stare. They exchanged quick, embarrassed smiles and turned their eyes away.

Rachel had to admit there was something fascinating about a woman who could sit patiently reading when at any moment all of her life forces could be called into action for the delivery of a child. For Rachel childbirth had been an awesome, turbulent experience, something for which she had conscientiously prepared her entire mind and body, right down to the nerve endings. But when Brian was born—when the pains had started and the waves and turbulence had swept over her—she had realized that no amount of preparation was quite enough. It had been a breech birth. Touch and go. Brian had come out a pallid blue and struggling for life. She could have lost him. She would never forget the cold terror of those harrowing moments.

But the woman across from Rachel appeared totally untroubled, as if she were quite ready to accept whatever pain or discomfort she would have to bear. Rachel envied her, for rarely could she herself sit back calmly and let things come as they would and pass over her. Somehow it was too important for Rachel to be in control, in the driver's seat, steering her life the way she felt it ought to go.

Not that she always steered so well, though!

Rachel shifted uncomfortably in her chair, willing the time away. It occurred to her she should pray for a negative report so she could get out of this crackerbox office and forget this absurd fear that she might be pregnant.

But what if she was pregnant? What then?

"David will have a fit," she said aloud.

Marlene rallied from her magazine. "What'd you say?"

"David—he's so involved in...in other things these days. One thing our marriage doesn't need is a baby!"

"It's a little late for regrets, isn't it?"

"It's too late for a lot of things." *Please, dear Lord, don't let it be,* Rachel willed silently. *Please don't let there be a baby!*

Marlene reached over and squeezed Rachel's hand. Her round, doughy face held a beatific shine. "Remember, gal, there's no problem too big for God. When my Harry died, I felt like I hit rock bottom. That's when I knew Christ was real. He took me by the hand and said, 'Honey, it's all right. You're going to be okay. Just walk with Me.'"

Rachel grimaced. "Might as well have asked you to walk on water or something."

"No, Rachel, even losing weight I don't imagine I could walk on water. But walking with Him *is* possible."

Rachel looked away. "I try to live my faith, Marlene, I really do. But lately it's hard enough just plodding through each day."

"Maybe you're trying too hard," said Marlene. "Following Jesus is so simple, so beautiful. Are you still digging into God's Word every day? And letting the Holy Spirit get hold of your life?"

"I try, but..." Rachel's words drifted off.

"Well, stop trying, gal," Marlene boomed, loud enough for everyone to hear, "and let God do it. Put your burdens on Him. His Son is a real person. Not just a man in history. We're not talking pie-in-the-sky religion here."

"Maybe we should talk about it later," Rachel suggested. She realized she was still holding the forms the receptionist had given her. She searched her purse for a pen and scribbled into the blank spaces the information requested. Name. Address. Telephone number. Insurance. She couldn't remember whether their insurance covered pregnancy. She would have to check with David. No, she would call the insurance company instead.

She laid the forms aside and glanced at her reflection in the oval mirror on the opposite wall, noting with relief that, in spite of her discomfiture, she looked intact, perhaps even attractive. Her makeup was correct. She had good eyes, she was confident of that. Clear cerulean blue, thickly lashed. Her brows were a trifle too arched and her mouth perhaps too full and wide to be pretty. But her medium-length honey brown hair had been done that morning. Jenny from the Carousel Beauty Salon did her hair each week, making the thick, tawny curls fall softly onto Rachel's forehead and caress her high cheekbones.

Even if she wasn't a classic beauty, David considered her pretty. And she was still young—wasn't she? Surely thirty-two couldn't be old—not these days when women even in their fifties were having babies. Long ago, when she and David were dating, he had told her she had the grace of a Madonna. He said no one walked with as much grace as she.

Rachel smiled inadvertently. Did David really say things like that once? It must have been some other lifetime, some other Rachel—the old Rachel. The girl she was when they were first married. The high school girl who could hardly wait for graduation, who less than two weeks later became Mrs. David Webber in one of those gaudy little wedding chapels in Las Vegas. That naive girl in rose-colored glasses had been gone for a long time, Rachel acknowledged mordantly.

Rachel shifted in her chair. Waiting for the nurse

to call her name was a royal pain. What was there to do but to think and remember? Or talk to Marlene. But Marlene had her nose buried in another magazine. With a sigh of resignation Rachel sat back and permitted the reels of memory to spin through her mind like old film clips.

She thought of Brian. What would he think about a baby? He was an awkward thirteen, a loner. He would be fourteen when the baby came—if a baby came. Hard to imagine that it was thirteen years since Brian had been born. Had it really been that long? She and David had been married only a year, and David had still had another year before he would receive his engineering degree from California State University at Long Beach. Rachel had had to give up her typing job and her cherished drama courses to take care of Brian, and David had taken a part-time job at night to pay the rent on their small Long Beach apartment.

''It's never been easy,'' Rachel murmured. She didn't realize she'd said the words aloud until Marlene looked up and asked what she had just said.

''Nothing important. Just thinking out loud.''

''So tell me.''

Rachel shrugged. ''To be honest, I was thinking how pleasant life was before Brian was born. David and I had so much fun our first year together—art lectures and films at the university, pizza parties with other students, drives to Solvang or San Diego. I remember our long walks around Knott's Berry Farm, munching popcorn as we peered in the windows of that old ghost town.''

''Sounds very romantic,'' Marlene mused. ''But a baby does change things.''

"Don't get me wrong, Marlene. We wanted Brian. We really did. But David and I rarely saw each other after his birth. David was in class all day or at the library studying. He'd come home for dinner before rushing off to his job at the garage, or grab a sandwich somewhere. I wouldn't see him until he collapsed into bed beside me long after midnight."

"And you think it'll be that way again, with a new baby?"

"Won't it? I don't think I could do it again, Marlene. I remember how tired I was—and depressed. Brian was a fussy, demanding baby. He kept me constantly on the run. He fretted when he was alone and was always into things. He screamed so much when I put him in the playpen I could barely take a shower or make a phone call."

"Didn't David help? Share some of the work?"

"David was always busy, preoccupied with his studies or work. On weekends he parked himself in front of the TV, watching football or baseball, or caught up on his sleep. He worked so hard all week, I guess I felt he had the right to do as he pleased on the weekend. I had to chase after Brian to keep him from disturbing his father."

"Surely things improved after David graduated," said Marlene.

"Yes, for a while. David landed a great engineering position in the aerospace industry and quit his evening job. He had regular hours and spent more time at home. Brian was older and more settled. And he sure loved to roughhouse with his dad."

"Wasn't Brian about three when you moved into the condo next door?"

Rachel nodded. "David was so excited when he

found that condo. We had finally saved enough money for a down payment on a house, but he wanted that flashy condo." Rachel sighed, remembering the brochure David had brought home. The development had been advertised as one of Southern California's most luxurious complexes, surrounded by palm trees, tropical shrubs and lush, blood red bougainvillea. It had the usual swimming pool, of course, and colored lights everywhere.

From the start Rachel had reservations about the condo. It wasn't suited to a growing family. The place gave off an artificial impression of opulence, but it wasn't practical or comfortable. Rachel would have preferred buying a larger but less ostentatious house—maybe a roomy old Victorian fixer-upper with a large yard and a picket fence in a settled section of Long Beach. But why mention it again? Marlene had heard it all before. A house would have provided room to stretch and grow, where Brian could play ball and fly kites, where they could plant a vegetable garden and rosebushes, and raise collie puppies and maybe even a couple of Angora kittens.

But David had a thousand reasons why the condo was a better buy. It was new and impressive and practically maintenance free. It was in an upper-scale neighborhood and yet close to the freeway, and it wouldn't depreciate as quickly as an old house in a declining neighborhood. And the condo would be easier to unload if the economy took another downturn, he told her, in case they were forced to relocate out of state. His firm relied on government contracts to survive, and David worried constantly about losing a job if the news reported the slightest dip in the economy. "In this life it's best to remain flexible," David told her time and again. "Travel light. Don't carry too much baggage. Be ready to pull up stakes, if necessary. Don't sink your roots in too deeply or you'll find yourself stuck in a rut."

Well, for all David's platitudes, she felt as if they were most definitely stuck in a rut. They had lived in the same condo for ten years now. Sometimes, particularly on Sunday afternoons, they would go for a drive and stop to look at model homes. They would walk through the professionally decorated rooms, praising a painting or commenting on the rich teal green of the carpet or the exquisite pattern of the wallpaper. They would survey the fine assortment of family rooms and dens, playrooms and bonus rooms that many of the homes boasted. It was at such model homes that Rachel had seen the large walk-in closets—nearly as large as this very office—and the master bedrooms that were practically a home in themselves. On such excursions, David would remark, "One of these days we'll have a house like this, big and fancy as a palace...." Silently she would muse that she'd be happy with one of those old Victorian fixer-uppers or even an old farmhouse in the country. But lately, she realized, David had stopped talking about buying another home.

In fact, lately David seemed to be pulling away from Brian and her. She hated to admit it—wouldn't breathe a word of it to Marlene—but David's life was increasingly disconnected from theirs. Of course, they had gone their separate ways for years. But this was something else, something more.

Again the suspicions nagged her. What about David? What was he doing? What was going on? Or was she being crazy to wonder about him when there was really no reason? What was wrong with her that she doubted her own husband? *God forgive my suspicions!* she silently prayed.

But no matter what the problems now, Rachel reminded herself, *once* her marriage had been good. At least, until—when was it? When did she and David really begin to grow apart?

There was only one answer to that question, and she felt guilty even thinking it. It was after she met Marlene. When was that? Five, six years ago? Yes. Brian was nearly eight. Marlene moved into the condo next door, alone. Her husband had died of a heart attack several years before. They had no children.

In spite of her loss, Marlene was a generous, funny, wonderfully open person. She had a quality of love and warmth about her that drew Rachel. In this one plain, lovely, outspoken woman Rachel found the sympathetic understanding of a mother, big sister and friend.

It hadn't taken Rachel long to discover that Marlene had fascinating and deeply entrenched opinions about many things—what it meant to be a woman, a Christian woman; what her responsibilities were to herself and to others; what her relationship ought to be to God. Marlene had related her opinions one afternoon while they had coffee in Rachel's apartment.

Even now, sitting stiffly, impatiently in Dr. Oberg's waiting room, Rachel recalled Marlene's words—the quiet, direct way she'd spoken of Jesus Christ and His resurrection and His desire to live in a person's heart.

Rachel's amazement had turned to curiosity, then to hunger. Here was Christianity as she had never heard it before—beautiful, powerful, capable of giving life a meaning she had always wished for but never dreamed possible. It involved so many things she was familiar with—Jesus of Nazareth, Christmas and Easter. Things everyone knew about. But then, why hadn't anyone told her that religion was just the periphery, that the center of it all was Christ?

"Rachel, honey, Jesus got off that cross a long time ago," Marlene had assured her. "He's not lying in that tomb anymore. He's alive, He's God and He loves you."

Marlene had prayed with Rachel that day and led her like a child to Christ. For a long while after that, Rachel had felt the wonder of innocence and the amazement of childhood in her blood again. She was free, clean. Even her daily routine took on purpose. It had all been so good.

It was still good, Rachel noted silently, but things were different now. She couldn't deny that some of the sparkle was gone. The sheen of her brand-new faith had worn thin and faded with the passing of months and years.

It wasn't entirely Rachel's fault. If only her faith hadn't become a wedge in her marriage. If only David shared her faith instead of resenting it. If only he would encourage Brian's faith by attending church with them occasionally, things would be so different.

And now, in recent weeks, there were other things—vague, disturbing things Rachel hardly dared put into words: David's preoccupation, his aura of secretiveness when she questioned him about his activities. He inevitably brushed her off with an excuse that he worried about work.

But was it the truth? Or was her marriage in even

deeper trouble than she suspected? Could it be that David had found a new interest...*someone else?* Until now Rachel hadn't dared to put the thought into words.

She chastened herself for harboring such suspicions. But the nagging questions could not be erased. Rachel's mind wavered between two poles—the agony that her suspicions might be correct and a gnawing guilt over the fact that she did not trust her husband.

Was it any wonder she didn't want to face a pregnancy now? Marlene just didn't understand. How could Rachel bring another life into the tangled web of her marriage? It was all she could do to cope with David and Brian. And lately, she was hardly able to cope with anyone—or anything—at all.

"Mrs. Webber? Mrs. Webber! The doctor will see you now."

Rachel frowned, attempting to swing her thoughts back to the present, struggling to recognize the voice that spoke her name. Who called her? But of course—the nurse.

Marlene gave her a nudge. "That's you, gal."

Rachel tried to rise casually, but she felt herself on the verge of leaping from her chair. The rotund lady seated across the room glanced up momentarily from her book, a flicker of interest lighting behind her eyes. The two teenagers offered curious stares, and Rachel felt an inexplicable impulse to apologize for something, to say, at least, "Excuse me."

She said it with her eyes but kept her lips tightly closed as she met the starched woman's professional gaze, then passed through the open door to the examining room.

Twenty minutes later, wrapped in a disposable paper gown, Rachel sat facing Dr. Oberg, a tall, lanky man with a bountiful head of curly hair.

"Well," the mild-mannered physician declared brightly, "the results are in." He glanced at the slip of paper he held as if it were a cue card and, with a smile, informed her, "As you probably already suspected, the test was positive, Mrs. Webber."

"Positive?" she echoed. She felt the color rise in her cheeks. "Are you sure? Couldn't there be a mistake?"

"Oh, no, Mrs. Webber. My examination confirmed it. You are pregnant." He patted her hand gently, almost a fatherly gesture. "Is there a problem? It is *Mrs.*, isn't it?"

"Yes, but my husband and son—they'll be... surprised."

"Pleasantly, I hope."

"So do I."

"Do you have other family nearby...to offer support?"

Rachel averted her gaze. "No. My parents died in a car crash when I was a teenager. And my husband's family lives in a small town in Ohio. We rarely see them."

"I see," said Dr. Oberg. He studied her chart for a moment. "I notice your son was a breech birth. There's no reason to expect another breech, you know. We'll anticipate a normal, healthy pregnancy. Tell me, do you have any questions?"

Rachel shook her head, her mind numb.

"Well, then," said Dr. Oberg, resuming an air of formality, "if you'll check with my nurse on the way out for your next appointment..."

Moments later Rachel walked out of the office, dazed, telling herself, This can't be real. It must be someone's clever prank, a hoax. Pregnant! What would she tell David? *Surprise! We're going to have a baby. Just what our marriage needs.*

Marlene caught up with her on the sidewalk, breathless. "Rachel, honey, don't forget me."

"I'm sorry. I—"

"The test?"

"Positive. Oh, Marlene, how will I tell David?"

"Maybe...pray about it?"

"I can't. I'm past praying."

On the way home Rachel had a daring idea. She would not tell David anything at all. Not yet. Why stir up trouble? Why muddy the waters? It would be weeks yet before she began to show. Anything could happen. The future was anybody's guess. There was time to work on her marriage, to improve her relationship with David, to prepare him for this so-called "blessed event."

Yes! Why not? For the present her pregnancy would remain her secret.

Chapter Two

It was late October, cold and storm-cloudy. David Webber gazed for a few moments into the dusky, smog-tinged dreariness outside his office window, then turned his attention back to his computer and the work at hand. The prints for the anti-icing design for the new regional jet had to be ready for the customer by 5:00 p.m. He fished through his desk drawer for paper clips, but as usual, couldn't find anything when he wanted it. Rubber bands, pencils and erasers, scratch paper and marking pens. But no paper clips. Impatiently he slammed the desk drawer, saying something unintelligible under his breath.

David caught a glimpse of his scowling reflection in the expansive windows beyond his desk. He wasn't one to think often about his looks, but when he did he had to admit to a modicum of conceit. Although nearing his mid-thirties, he had managed to maintain his athletic physique. It helped, of course, having good genes and being over six feet tall. Weekends of tennis and jogging under a hot California sun had tanned his skin a deep reddish brown, giving him a rugged, weather-beaten, even seafaring appearance. Rachel used to tell him with an admiring smile that he looked like one of those macho film stars—he could never keep up with the names. Come to think of it, it had been ages since she'd said anything like that.

These days it was Kit Kincaid, the engineering secretary, who fed his ego with effusive praise. She had even teasingly remarked that it must have been his double in that ubiquitous TV ad showing a smiling, virile, more-than-handsome workman chugalugging a diet soda while the office girls swooned with admiration. The comment had secretly pleased David. He was glad Kit considered him handsome—a man's man and, yes, a woman's man.

He looked back at his desk. Paperwork was strewn about like gigantic pieces of confetti. Before David could make sense of the chaos, Ralph Mercer, one of the draftsmen, came striding his way. ''Webber, have you gone over the check prints of my drawing?''

''Which drawing?''

''Last Friday's. The top assembly for the anti-ice system,'' Ralph reminded him.

''Yeah, it's here—somewhere.'' He riffled through a mound of papers. ''Yes, here it is.'' He had merely set the Wellman test report on top of it. ''Look, I'll check the drawing once more and get it right back to you.''

The draftsman left abruptly, only slightly mollified.

David scanned the drawing, remembering now that everything was all right. If the draftsman had waited a minute, he could have taken the check print with him. Now David would have to deliver it personally.

Irritated, he wrapped the check print around a roll of vellums for the Hiller job. Might as well deliver everything at once.

Casually he aimed his vision at Kit's desk. With her curly, honey blond hair tousled around her ivory-smooth face, she looked younger than her twenty-five years. He'd never have guessed they'd become such close friends. Yet Kit had a certain mature, even worldly outlook that had impressed David from the start. She was easy to talk with and he always felt relaxed and more positive about life in her company. Once Rachel's company had made him feel that way. But those days were long gone, he reflected sadly.

Kit was typing something, unaware of his gaze. With drawings in hand he headed for her desk. Paper clips were a good excuse—a reason to interrupt her work, talk to her, make her smile.

"Talk a minute?" he asked when she looked up, startled.

She smiled. "Okay, David. Sure."

He lowered his voice a degree and assumed what he considered a tone of stern authority. "Miss Kincaid, you are the secretary to the engineering department, are you not?"

She studied him with a curious half smile. "You know I am."

"Then you, my dear, are responsible for keeping us supplied with such indispensable items as paper clips, right?"

"Yes, I suppose so...."

"Now I must warn you, Miss Kincaid, if you forsake these small but important duties, you'll only go on to greater negligence in the future."

She stifled a laugh. "Come on, David. Are you out again? What do you do? Eat them?"

He winked. "Sure. It gives me an excuse to talk to you."

Her voice softened. "Since when do you need an excuse, David?"

He inhaled sharply. "All right, young lady, give me six boxes now, or I'll find your supply and pilfer the entire stock. Then where will you be?"

She leaned toward him and raised her face to his. "Right here, where I want to be. With you."

She looked delightfully impish, as if there were many wonderful secrets locked in her head, which she would share only when she chose to, with whom she chose.

"Here are your paper clips," she announced brightly, removing a small cardboard box from her desk. "Are you planning to make me a necklace?"

"Yeah, but not out of paper clips." He fumbled with the drawings he forgot he was holding. "Say, Kit," he added softly, making his voice sound as if they were still talking about paper clips. "Kit, how would you like to get a bite to eat after work?"

Her face showed surprise. "Tonight? Don't you need to be home?"

Although they'd had lunch together a few times, David had never before asked to spend time with her after work. As he observed her reaction, he felt surprised himself at what he'd done and almost hoped she'd turn him down.

"I just phoned Brian a few minutes ago, and he said Rachel is out shopping. He doesn't know when she'll get back." He thrummed his fingers on her desk. "So I told him I have to work late. I thought we'd at least have time to grab a sandwich. But if you'd rather not..."

"No, that's all right. I'd like to. But I'll have to call my roommate. She thought I'd be home. She was going to try something fancy for dinner. A soufflé or something. She won't want to bother just for herself. I'll just let her know I won't be joining her."

"I'm sorry I couldn't let you know sooner."

"That's okay. I'm just glad for the chance to be with you. You know that."

"Yeah, me, too." He glanced around guardedly. "Meet you in the parking lot, okay?"

"Sure."

David delivered the check print and vellums, then returned to his desk and shuffled idly through the odds and ends of paperwork—government specifications, purchase orders and engineering estimate forms. He worked mindlessly with the paper clips, attaching them to the corners of papers, but his eyes—and his thoughts—remained on Kit across the room. Finally, to appear occupied, he scanned the current issue of *Aviation Week*.

After work, because their time together was so limited, David drove Kit to the nearby Hamburger House, where they took a back booth and ordered promptly. This place was perfect, only blocks from Kit's apartment and halfway between work and David's condo. It was a spot usually crowded at this hour with the after-five teenage traffic from the nearby junior college. It was a place where the two of them could be unnoticed, ignored, lost in the crowd.

As he sipped his cola, David watched several teenagers swaying to a rock tune, their limber bodies graceful as velvet sashes strung in the breeze. His son,

Brian, was a teenager now. One day a child you could wrestle with and jounce in the air. One day a child, and the next... Now Brian was reaching into another world. Perhaps he would be swept up like all the other kids his age, forced to join and conform or to test and try the limits. Most likely, he would attempt to defy the established order of things. It was expected these days.

Still, it startled David to find himself massing his son with all the others—the rebels, the freaks, even the majority of good kids who still experimented with one thing or another. Morals were like that now. Everyone saw what he wanted to see, even David. He did what he pleased, stretched the limits and rearranged the boundaries. Brian would be no different—no better and no worse.

"Are you coming back soon?"

"What?"

Kit was sitting across from him in the booth, beaming, a peculiar half smile on her polished red lips. "I said, if you don't come back soon from wherever you've wandered, I'm going to steal your dill pickle and carrot sticks."

"Be my guest."

"Where were you?"

"Thinking about Brian."

"Is he in some kind of trouble?"

David grimaced. Not as much as I am. "No, not at all," he said with a note of defensiveness. Why had he even mentioned Brian? Now he felt compelled to assure Kit everything was fine. "He loves eighth grade. He's doing well. No complaints from anyone, as far as I know."

"Well, then?"

David hated being put on the spot. "I was—I don't know—just imagining him being like these kids. They're a whole new breed."

"And it's hard to picture Brian being one of them, right?"

He shrugged. "He's my son. I love him."

"He'll do okay. From what you've told me, he's a great kid."

"He is," David agreed, shaking steak sauce on his sandwich.

"I wish I could meet him."

David glanced up, startled. He felt his neck muscles tighten. "I wish you could, too, Kit. But it's just not possible. You know that."

Kit flushed. "David, I'm sorry. I didn't mean anything. It was just an idle remark. I'm not trying to push you. Really, I'm not."

"I know, Kit. I'm sorry. I get wound up sometimes and shoot off my big mouth."

"But I know I don't make things any easier for you."

"It's not your fault. It's just the way things are."

"For what it's worth, David, I adapt easily," she said. "If a friendship is it—just what we have now—fine. If more comes, that's fine, too. If not, I understand. Do you know what I'm saying, David?"

"I know what you're saying, Kit. And I know you understand. I guess that's why I like being with you so much. But relationships aren't static. They grow and change. They take on a life of their own," he added, thinking about his own marriage as much as his friendship with Kit.

She traced a water ring with one long, polished nail. "Like you've said before, we'll just take our time...and see what happens."

Chapter Three

The late October sky was rain swollen and color streaked. It had not started to storm yet, but it would, and soon. As Rachel aimed her teal green sedan homeward through late-afternoon traffic, she tried to imagine how the evening would be. After two weeks of guarded silence, tonight she would tell David about the baby. Before he arrived home, she would toss a salad and put in potatoes to bake. Then she would cook fresh broccoli and broil the porterhouse steaks she had just purchased at a special butcher shop. She had forgotten to pick up sour cream, but she could whip up David's favorite cheese sauce, and there were fresh mushrooms in the refrigerator. Perhaps they could even eat by candlelight, or was that considered gauche now? She would decide later.

Once dinner was started, Rachel thought she would change into something else, perhaps one of her long gauzy skirts that David liked so much. She hardly wore them lately. She would wait until they had eaten—probably wait even until Brian was in bed—

before telling him about the baby. She would be calmer; so would he. They would discuss things intelligently. Perhaps it would not really be so bad. Perhaps a baby would not be a catastrophe after all.

But on entering the condo, Rachel felt an immediate surge of irritation. Brian was home, sprawled on the sofa, staring impassively at the six-o'clock pro football game on television, his heavy hiker boots propped on her glass coffee table. And he was scarfing down greasy potato chips, the crumbs scattering all over her rose velvet sofa. His straight, light-brown hair spilled over his high, ruddy forehead, shading his heavy-lidded hazel eyes. He was wearing a striped rugby shirt and baggy jeans. He looked up from the flickering screen and must have sensed her displeasure, for he swung his feet to the floor and moved the bag of chips to the coffee table.

She forced the irritation out of her voice, inquiring, "Have you been home long, Brian?"

His wide, chiseled mouth settled into a pout. "Yeah, a little while."

"You came right home from school then?"

"Uh-huh."

Rachel set down her purse and removed her suede patchwork jacket, her annoyance lingering. "I thought maybe you'd be out with your friends."

"Naw, they got soccer practice." It was still a sore point that he hadn't made the team. He hesitated. "I was wondering though," he began, a sudden lilt in his voice. "I met this guy at school today, Ronnie Mayhew. He's ahead of me—in the ninth grade. He's a real cool guy, Mom, and I wondered if he could come over tonight? He's going to bring some of his CDs."

"You want someone over tonight, Brian?" Rachel's mind raced. Tonight had to be special, and there was still so much to do. She stalled. "This is a school night, remember?"

"Yeah, but Ronnie's mom said he can come if it's all right with you. He found this cool chat room on the Internet, and—"

"You know I don't like you surfing the Internet. You don't know who's out there."

"Come on, Mom, it's totally safe. Would you rather have me out on the streets, hanging out or something?"

She stared him down. "I'd rather have you here in your own room doing your homework. Especially your algebra."

"It's done, Mom. No lie! I did it in my free period. So can Ronnie come over?"

"Oh, Brian, please!"

"Listen, Mom, most of the time ninth graders don't even want to hang out with guys in eighth grade." Her son sat up, leaning forward, his neck and arms angular, his shoulders taut, as if somehow he had to impress upon her physically the importance of his request. She chose to ignore it.

"Brian—Brian, not tonight, please. Maybe tomorrow. Ask him for tomorrow night."

The boy scowled. "Yeah, sure. He probably won't want to come then."

"Then he's not much of a friend."

"Aw, Mom, come off it."

"That's enough, Brian." Rachel wasn't winning this one at all. She didn't want to contend with Brian now when there was so much on her mind, so much to do, to plan. She had already endured a couple of weeks of morning sickness, hiding out in the bathroom until David left for work so he wouldn't guess the truth. She'd finally had enough of covering up her condition. She was determined to tell David tonight. But should she take Brian into her confidence? It might help to have him as her ally. She looked at him, searching his face, and wondered for a moment just who her son was now.

Last year, when Brian was twelve, he'd seemed small to Rachel; his face was plain and round, unmarked, still sweet, a child's face. His body was still child-like soft and smooth. Young girls and boys seemed alike, all soft and smooth. They all had untouched faces, open and wide and wondering.

Now Brian was thirteen, and already his face had begun to close, to change, to take on new facets and meanings somewhere behind the eyes. Now his body was suddenly stretching, breaking through the softness, making angles of his arms and legs. In just one year a shrewdness and a new curiosity had registered on his face, around his mouth.

As if to confirm the unseen changes, Brian's face was no longer smooth. Hints of pimples appeared on his chin and forehead. He was becoming someone Rachel wondered if she knew. It was too soon for this sort of thing, too soon. The changes, coming so fast, left Rachel a little bewildered at times, confused as to how she should handle her son. Should she treat him as a child? As a man? He was Brian, whoever Brian was becoming. But she could not think of Brian now.

She sat down beside him and put the potato chip bag on her lap. She rolled the slick edges of the bag between her fingers, unaware she was doing so.

"Brian," she said, "I didn't want to go into this until I talked with your father, but I guess there's no reason you can't know now."

"Know what, Mom?" He had slouched back against the cushions, his hazel eyes impassive, watching her.

"Do you remember when I went to the doctor's for a checkup a couple of weeks ago? Well, I found out...I found out I'm going to have a baby."

He sat up, suddenly alert. The amazement in his voice was genuine. "You're kidding, Mom."

"No, I'm afraid not."

His wide mouth curled at one corner. "A baby? That's really something. I mean, I never thought of a baby. You aren't too old or anything?"

Rachel's irritation was returning. "No, I'm not too old," she snapped. Then, more softly, "But it was a surprise to me, too."

"Does Dad know?" he quizzed eagerly.

Rachel shook her head. "No, I haven't told him yet."

"Boy, will he be flipped out. When are you going to tell him?"

"I'll tell him tonight, after dinner. That's why I'd rather your friend come over another time."

"Yeah, sure. Okay," he said, nodding, then added, "But Dad won't be home for dinner."

A knot of disappointment tightened in her chest. "Why not?"

"He called a while go. I told him you were out shopping. He said he had to work late. Said he'd grab a bite on the way home."

"Great." She sighed. *There goes my porterhouse-steaks-and-candlelight plan,* she thought. She knew she should have called David at the office to see if he'd be home at his usual time, but she'd had no chance.

"We still gotta eat," Brian reminded her.

Rachel felt deflated. Her energy had vanished. "How about a hamburger?"

"Rad. How about the Hamburger House, where Dad takes us sometimes? They have great shakes."

She was too tired to argue. "All right, if you get the food to go. I don't feel like going in."

Dutifully, her spirits ebbing, Rachel drove Brian to the Hamburger House and waited in the car while he went in for hamburgers, shakes and fries. She sat with the window rolled partly down, her polished fingernails lightly tapping the leather-wrapped steering wheel, her eyes momentarily catching a glimpse of passing strangers. She focused briefly on a gas station being torn down across the street, then turned her gaze to the restaurant's neatly lettered window signs advertising the special of the week: Fudge Sundae Delight, with whipped cream and nuts.

The sky had remained the same. Dusky gray clouds ready to burst into drenching rain hovered overhead, swollen and heavy like a great woman in waiting, as she herself would be in time. Why didn't it just rain and get it over with? Why did things have to stand still, horribly, oppressively still?

Rachel's mind was somewhere else, her thoughts wandering, so she might have missed David and the girl entirely. At first she only vaguely realized it was David coming out the door, David and a young girl who looked familiar and yet was a stranger.

Rachel's first impulse was to call out to her husband, to say, "Here I am, David. Funny to run into you here.'' The impulse was squelched immediately by something else, a dread, a terrible feeling of being trapped in a bad dream. David was walking with some girl—a pretty, stylishly dressed blonde. Who was she? Why were they together? He was supposed to be at the office, working late.

Could Rachel be wrong? Could the man be someone who only looked like David? No. She watched as they strolled to a vehicle and climbed in. It was David's fiery red sports car with the auto club sticker on the bumper. No doubt about it. The man was David. The way they had walked, the two of them, with a close, companionable air, her cheek nearly brushing his shoulder, and the way his hand touched her waist as he helped her into the car suggested there was something between them. They looked comfortable together, more than friendly; totally focused on each other in an intense way that filled Rachel's heart with cold dread.

Rachel could feel it like a shock. They were more than acquaintances. Maybe even more than friends. There was something heavy going on, and the knowledge of it shot through Rachel's body like hot gunfire, leaving her wrists and ankles weak. Without a word, with only an unintended glimpse, her worst suspicions had been confirmed and the plain facts made her numb. Her husband had strayed. Had found someone else. And while Rachel's world reeled and spun around her, David and the girl simply got into his car and drove away without once seeing Rachel there at all.

Chapter Four

"Are you hungry, David?" Rachel asked, watching her husband with cool, careful eyes.

"No," he said. He was loosening his tie, pulling it off from around his neck. He looked weary but unruffled, his charcoal gray suit impeccable, his handsome features as boyishly appealing as ever. There was nothing to suggest this night wasn't the same as every other night. "Where's Brian?"

"In his room, studying."

"Is there any cold soda in the fridge?"

"I don't know. You can check."

"How about you? You check, okay? I'm bushed."

"All right." Rachel went to the kitchen and returned to the living room with an open can of cola. David took it, drank and set the can on a coaster on the coffee table. He unbuttoned his shirt, found the evening newspaper, the *Press-Telegram,* and sat down in his chair, the nubby, adobe-brown recliner that was adjustable to several positions. Rachel hated that chair. It was an eyesore amid her elegant Queen

Anne chairs and velvet sofa. But David didn't care. He seemed to take a perverse delight in keeping his recliner in a prominent place in the living room. Even now, he tilted back expansively and opened his paper with a self-satisfied flourish.

"I heard the stock market went down again today, more than a hundred points," he said from behind the paper, his voice sounding as if he weren't really talking to anyone in particular and didn't care whether he got a reply.

"Really?" she murmured distractedly.

"Of course, the economists are saying it's a normal market correction," he mused. "But one of these days it's going to plunge again and take us all to the cleaners. Maybe we should be pumping more of my 401K savings into bonds instead of stocks. What do you think?"

When Rachel didn't reply, he went on, as if talking to himself. "It's not like things have completely recovered in aerospace. The bottom could fall out again, you know, and where would we be?" He took another drink, then set the can back into the coaster. "They laid off three guys in manufacturing last week, three of them, and I mean they were top guys, right up there. Trouble is, there's not enough work. We've lost out on several big contracts lately. I say management's to blame. We've got clients beating a path to the competition. I tell you, if I were running the show, I'd make some real changes."

For a moment he became absorbed in an item in the paper. When he spoke again, he picked up the same thread of conversation. "Of course, no one's asking me what I think. I guess I should just be grateful no one's taken a hatchet to my job."

Sitting silently on the sofa, her legs crossed comfortably, listening to David ramble on amiably, Rachel wondered if her mind might be playing tricks on her. This was just like any other night, like every night. David in his chair, having a soda, reading the paper, talking about work and the economy and what was happening to whom. It was all very natural, very right. Only it wasn't right, not when she forced her mind to remember the afternoon, the crazy, mixed-up afternoon.

Surely she hadn't seen David today with another woman, some mysterious girl, someone he seemed to know so well, whom she, Rachel, didn't know at all. Certainly nothing existed except tonight, this moment, everything orderly, quiet and in its place. Should she shatter this peace? Should she force the issue, the issues—David and the girl, the baby, the whole vague, uncertain direction of their lives? Was she really up to all that? She could keep her mouth shut and go to bed. Shut up and sleep and sleep and sleep. But then things would be no different tomorrow.

"David," she began tentatively. Her face felt strained, her mouth screwed up too tight to speak. "David," she said again, "how come if things are so bad with the company they have you working overtime so much?"

He set the paper down and gave her a blank look. "What do you mean by that?"

"I just wondered, that's all."

"I have a lot to do. They give me work the other guys used to do, the guys they laid off."

"I see." Her voice was the size of a pinprick, light, airy.

David gave her a second look, close, scrutinizing.

"Is something wrong, Rae?" He called her that sometimes. "Are you all right?"

"Sure. I had a bad day, I guess." Might as well plunge ahead, might as well. "Something funny happened, David," she said. "I can't figure it. I saw you today, David, but you didn't see me."

David's expression stayed the same, his eyes watching her, but something in his face seemed to change, shift. "You did? Where?"

"At the Hamburger House. We—Brian and I—went there for dinner. We took food out. We came home and ate."

"The Hamburger House?" A light came on in David's eyes, a dazed brightness, as if his mind were weighing many things at once, so that he could not yet speak. Finally he said, "What were you doing at the Hamburger House?"

Rachel looked at him, surprised. "I just told you. Brian and I—"

"Oh, yes, I know that, but I mean...well, why didn't you say something if you saw me?"

"You were busy, David. You were with someone."

As if light had dawned, David broke into an extravagant laugh. "Oh, you mean Kit. You saw me with Kit Kincaid." He settled back and picked up his paper again, as if by such a gesture he was dismissing a topic too insignificant to pursue. From behind the paper his voice flowed evenly, nonchalant. "Kit is the secretary in our department. Her car wasn't running so I gave her a ride home. Neither of us had eaten, and it was getting late, so we picked up a sandwich. You should have called us, Rachel. You should have said something."

She shrugged uncertainly. "You looked so engrossed, so close somehow, I felt like an outsider. I felt—" Rachel was aware of her voice growing quivery all of a sudden. She thought she might cry. Was it relief? What? "I didn't mean to sound stupid, David, like a suspicious wife or something. It's just that I had a big dinner planned, and then there you were—"

"I called and said I had to work, baby."

"I know you did." She felt suddenly stupid, tongue-tied. "But it seems like you have to work so much lately, and I had this idea about tonight being special." On impulse, she got up and went over to David, slipping onto the arm of his chair, letting her arm circle his shoulder, resting lightly, carefully. "I guess I couldn't stand seeing you look so happy with that girl. I mean, you really looked...happy."

"Rachel, will you stop it! Stop hounding me. I told you what happened. I'm sorry you were upset."

Rachel eased her body off the chair arm, going down on her knees, sitting like a silly, foolish schoolgirl. She was looking at her husband as if she might be begging, as if she might be screaming for something inside, screaming against the complete silence of her mouth, her lips.

David's hand, large and manly, came to rest on Rachel's shoulder, found the back of her neck and rubbed gently, soothingly. "I didn't mean to shout, Rae. Really, I'm sorry. It's just that I don't like you going on like this about Kit."

"Are you...in love with her?" This a whisper, hardly spoken, this from Rachel who could not believe she had asked it.

The directness of the question took David by surprise. He said unthinkingly, "I don't know."

The two of them had been sitting in a calm, orderly room surrounded by handsomely elegant, well-placed furniture, with soft light emanating from quiet lamps and everything proper, in its place, where it belonged. This room, one segment of their condo, was fine, and she and David had been fine until this moment, having a serious but comprehensible discussion.

Now nothing was right at all, and nothing Rachel could do would make it right. In a moment, less than a moment, neither the room nor David nor Rachel made any sense at all.

It was bizarre, this conversation. It was idiotic, the whole thing. What was she doing asking David about being in love with another woman?

"Well, you asked me," David said defensively, seeing the look on her face. "You asked me, so I figured you knew. You asked if I love her, and I told you the truth. I don't know. You want me to play it straight with you, don't you, Rae?"

"I didn't know anything!" she railed, the very breath snatched from her lungs. "I don't know why I said that, why I asked if you love her. I d-didn't know—" She was drowning in a welter of confusion and could only stammer that she really didn't know anything at all.

He stared at her. "You mean, you really didn't have any idea about Kit? Then why in the world did you bring it up? Why did you have to push me, Rachel? Why couldn't you leave things alone?"

Her head spun, the lamplight blinding her. "I don't know...."

David put a tentative hand on her shoulder, then

removed it. "I didn't want to hurt you, Rachel. I could have lied. I started to! You know I don't want to hurt you."

"I know," she said, not looking at him, not seeing anything, still dazed, groping with a blizzard of conflicting thoughts whirling in her own head.

"Hang it all anyway," David said, his brows knitting over dark flashing eyes. "This whole world is going down the drain, you know that? I'm going down the drain, and the whole world, too. What's the use of anything?"

Hearing this new torment in David's voice, Rachel snapped out of her own preoccupation. Her mind was clearing fast. "David," she said, "talk to me. We've got to talk about this. I have to understand what's happening."

"What's the use? I mean, really, what's the use of anything?"

"I have to understand this, David." She felt a sudden urge to reach out and touch him but she held back. Instead, she got up from the floor and went over to the sofa and sat down. It was a lovely sofa, the color of spring roses, but there were crumbs from potato chips on it, and she brushed them off. Certainly, she thought, some of these things that had happened could be undone, brushed aside like crumbs, forgotten. She had to find out where she and David stood. "David," she said, forcing her voice to remain calm, "tell me what's going on."

He had the newspaper again, rolling it up, twisting and turning it, unaware that he was destroying it with his very hands. "I don't know what to say, Rachel," he said, his hands busy with the paper. "What can I say? I mean, Kit and I have gotten to be good friends.

We didn't plan anything. We just hit it off, you know. Things sort of clicked...."

"When was this?"

"A couple of months ago, I guess. Late in the summer."

Rachel forced herself to ask the question that seared her heart. "Are you having an affair, David?"

A flash of surprise and indignation crossed David's face. "No. No, Rachel. Believe me, it hasn't gone that far. I wouldn't. We're friends. Special friends, I guess. We see each other now and then, for lunch. This was the first time we've ever met after work, but I guess you won't believe that."

"You're right, I don't," Rachel replied in a flat tone.

Suddenly he slammed the paper down on the table, jarring a crystal dish that sat on its polished surface. "I shouldn't be telling you this," he said. "I must be crazy saying anything at all. I must be crazy."

Rachel's heart hammered. She felt the pressure of tears behind her eyes. "I need to know, David," said Rachel. "Everything. It's only fair...."

Her husband grew quiet, apparently gathering his thoughts. He leaned forward in his chair, his shoulders slumping, round and heavy, his eyes focused somewhere in space. He massaged his knuckles. "You know yourself, Rachel," he said in a small, tight voice, "things haven't been good between us for a long time. You know that."

Tears glazed her eyes. "We've had our problems, yes...."

He looked at her, his eyes glinting with fire. "Problems? Problems? You bet we've had problems. I'm not excusing myself, believe me, I'm not, but...I guess it seemed like an escape to be interested in someone else for a while. It was harmless, Rachel, really.''

''But you said—'' Her tongue felt thick, pasty, her voice a whisper. ''You said you don't know if you love this girl, this Kit. You said you don't know.''

He shook his head. ''I—I don't know.''

Rachel inhaled sharply. She couldn't hear her own voice over her thundering heart. ''But you might... you might love her?''

David stared hard at his hands. ''I just don't know,'' he said.

Chapter Five

"Hey, Dad, when did you get home?"

It was Brian, bounding into the living room full of a boy's endless energy, grinning broadly at his dad, his enthusiasm noisy. Lately, it seemed Brian was often this way around his dad, almost joyous, sharing something private, something Rachel couldn't quite touch. But why did he have to come in now?

Dear God, why now?

"Hey, man! How's it going?" David responded brightly, obviously glad to be off the hook with Rachel for a moment. "I got home a while ago. How about you? What's the word?"

"Nothing, Dad. Hitting the books is all. Doing some research on the Internet. History report. No big deal."

"School's always a big deal."

"Sure, if you say so."

David chuckled. "You'll change your tune one of these days."

"Yeah, yeah, I know. But, hey, how about you? Mom tell you the news?"

Rachel saw David flinch slightly. His smile froze on his lips. "What do you mean, Brian? Tell me what?"

The words burst from Brian's lips. "About the baby. You told him, Mom, didn't you?"

Rachel scarcely breathed. "No, Brian." She was losing the modicum of control she had over this situation. She didn't want it to be like this. Everything was collapsing around her. "I haven't had a chance, Brian. I was going to—"

David pulled himself out of his recliner and stood in the middle of the room as if he were not sure what he should do next. "What is this?" he said. "Rachel, tell me what's going on."

She glared at her son. "Brian, go to your room and let me talk to Daddy, would you please?"

"Okay, Mom." He looked at both of them apologetically. "I'm sorry if I spoiled the surprise. I mean, I figured you already told him."

As Brian left the room, Rachel steeled herself. It was her trump card, this baby, but she didn't want to play it now. She didn't want to hold on to David this way, if there was anything left of their marriage to hold together.

David stood across from her, his body steeled, too, and minced no words. "Rachel, are you pregnant?"

"Yes."

"In the name of heaven, why didn't you tell me? What kind of game are you playing?"

"You're a good one to talk about playing games," she countered, wishing immediately she hadn't retaliated.

"Oh, we're back to that, are we?" David made a helpless gesture with his hands and sat down. "Rachel," he said solemnly, "what do you want me to do?"

Rachel stared down at her hands. "I don't know, David. You tell me. What do you want to do?"

He shook his head. "I don't know what to do, what to think. I suppose we have to go on from here, from this moment. We've got to pull things together, you and I. Especially now."

She spoke with a bitter irony. "You mean, for the baby?"

"Yes, I mean for the baby. For Brian, too. For all of us."

It was not in Rachel now to respond coolly, to debate and discuss their lives with objectivity. She resented David's attempt to settle their lives by logic. Didn't he understand, couldn't he see, that she was coming apart inside? He wanted to talk about tangible things, about plans, about doing this or that. Rachel was concerned with only one intangible, terribly important fact: David evidently no longer loved her, and he might love—actually might love—somebody else.

"Are you listening to me, Rachel? Didn't you hear anything I said?"

"Yes, David, I heard you, but it's too late!" Didn't everything inside tell her it was too late? All the terrible particles of herself coming apart—the torn bits and pieces of her logical mind, whatever that was, if she'd ever possessed such a thing. Everything inside her was ready to revolt, and she thought she might vomit. She stood as if to head for the bathroom.

"Are you all right?" David asked. "Are you sick, Rachel?"

"I don't know—no, I'm all right. I'm a little dizzy, that's all."

"You should go to bed. Rae, let me help you." David made a gesture toward her, which she rejected as quickly as it was made. He withdrew, letting her pass by him.

"I'm all right," she said, waving her hand, dismissing him. "I have to be alone, David. I've got to think. I just can't think tonight."

He shook his head, his voice heavy with regret. "I'm sorry, Rachel. I really am. I'm sorry for this whole mess."

She turned and stared at him. The urge to cry was on her again, washing over her like warm water, like wonderfully warm rivers that might drown her. But she held back the tears, the desire to let herself weep in David's arms. Instead, she asked, "What about her—this girl?"

"I don't know. I'll have to break it off," David answered.

"But your feelings. You said you don't know how you feel."

"I'll work it out, Rachel. It'll be okay."

She didn't want to hear this. It wasn't the answer she needed. "Don't bother, David," Rachel said, her voice suddenly high and strangled. "Don't bother with charity. I don't want any of it. I just want you out of here. Get out of here—please!" She held the sobs inside herself, the pressure building like a stone in her throat.

David's mouth tightened as a dazed, incredulous expression settled in his eyes. He was obviously shaken. Could he go so easily, without a fight? For a moment she thought he would argue with her, refuse to leave, even plead with her to let him stay. But she knew he was too proud and hated to appear weak, no matter what. "All right, Rachel," he said, already moving heavily, dispiritedly toward their room. "I'll pack a bag and get out. I'll go, if that's what you want."

"Yes," she said, turning away, going to the window, hugging herself protectively. She was trembling like a rosebud in a tempest.

It was raining finally. The rain poured down and hit the window outrageously, like torrents of tears, like the sudden furious tears in her own eyes.

Chapter Six

Three days after David had gone striding out of their apartment, suitcase in hand and jaw set, Rachel broke out of her self-imposed mourning. It was a balmy, sun-washed day, and she needed to get out.

Not that she could escape the scorching recriminations, the self-pity, blaming herself one moment for her impulsiveness, resenting David the next for actually walking out at her insistence. As if that's what she wanted, his going. Was it? Who knew? All she knew at the moment, on this breezy, clear day in early November, was that she had to get out of herself, out of the house, away. So she and Marlene drove to Laguna Beach to spend the day.

Laguna was one of their favorite places. Somehow the endless clusters of quaint, colorful buildings perched on the hillsides and the little network of streets had managed to escape that steely, glazed look that had become the characteristic of so much of Southern California. Rachel was tired of the endless stark, cold ribbons of freeway twisting and turning, jutting in and out, stripping the landscape of any natural grace.

Laguna Beach was different. The buildings were clever and original. They looked as if they had a history to them, as if many people had given parts of their personalities to these structures. The colorful little shops were crowded with artists' paintings—lovely seascapes, beautiful landscapes, portraits and still lifes.

Many artists came here hoping to sell their work, the trained and untrained alike. Rachel adored their paintings, the meticulous portraits of old men from the sea, children in soft, airy dresses, and the tiny, finely crafted canvases of fruit—a single apple or a pear, stark against an ebony background.

Throughout the afternoon, Rachel knew Marlene was bursting with unasked questions. Marlene said nothing but cast frequent sidelong glances at Rachel, no doubt to determine the state of her emotions. Marlene was too kind to bombard her with probing queries about David's sudden move out of their condo. On the phone the morning after David left, Rachel had spilled out the story in brief choked snatches, leaving it to Marlene to fill in the blanks.

"He's gone and that's all there is to it, Marlene," Rachel had told her friend that morning. "And I don't want to talk about it anymore. I just can't."

So that was it. Rachel had said no more.

But now Rachel felt better. Relaxed by the pleasant day at Laguna and with her emotions lulled by gentle sea breezes, she felt capable of discussing with some degree of objectivity her present circumstances. She told Marlene everything that came to her mind as they drove home that evening, finishing with "Yesterday

I called a lawyer over in north Long Beach. I had a long talk with him and he suggested I come in for an appointment.''

"You're not really going, are you?''

"I'm thinking about it.''

"Does that mean you're thinking about getting a divorce?''

Rachel struggled to keep her tone neutral. "I have to consider it. I just didn't realize how things are these days, with the divorce laws and all. The lawyer told me that under California law it's not a divorce anymore. It's a *dissolution.* All you have to say is that you have irreconcilable differences, and that's it, you can have your divorce. It's just about that easy. You merely have to wait six months, for what he called the interlocutory period, then the whole thing is done with.'' Rachel's voice wavered with ill-disguised emotion. "What do you think of that?''

"It sounds ghastly to me,'' said Marlene, feigning a shudder. She was driving, and they were on the freeway now, in the fast lane, going sixty-five. Marlene liked to drive and could handle a car as well as anyone. She could drive anywhere, for hours at a time, and not get tired or nervous. When she and Rachel went anywhere, Rachel always let her drive.

"The whole thing sounds awful to me, too,'' Rachel admitted with a flat little smile, actually more grimace than smile. She recalled the lawyer's voice, smooth and silky, unconcerned. "While I was talking to the lawyer I thought I must be out of my mind. Here I was talking about David and myself with some stranger like it was nothing at all.

"Anyhow, he said with the laws like they are these days, there's less recrimination and guilt. He kept using those words, recrimination and guilt. There's no blaming anyone, he said. He claims that makes it all a lot easier."

Rachel paused and sighed audibly. The sigh seemed to go all the way through her, somehow snatching her strength, leaving her tired. "There's nothing easy about tearing up a whole part of your life and throwing it away," she said. "He made it sound as easy as wrapping up the garbage and taking it out."

"I just hope you don't go and do anything on impulse, Rachel," warned Marlene. "Divorce, that should be a last resort."

"Well, the lawyer said you have to pay at least half the fee as soon as you start divorce proceedings. I guess a lot of people get halfway through and change their minds, so the lawyer would be out a lot, I suppose, if he didn't have you pay at the start. Anyway, I don't want to do anything until I'm absolutely sure."

Marlene's voice took on a cautionary note. "I was just wondering—have you prayed about all this, Rachel?"

Rachel mindlessly twisted her purse strap around her index finger. "Everything's happened so fast I haven't had much chance to pray," she admitted lamely. She didn't want to confess that at the moment the thought of praying left her with a terrified, strangled sensation. "I won't do anything without praying about it first," she assured Marlene, her voice rising a degree, "so don't worry about that." But how could she convince Marlene when she couldn't even convince herself?

Marlene looked over at her, her round face clouding. "It's just that...well, I have this feeling about you, Rachel."

"What? What feeling?"

"I don't know. You're putting me on the spot—I can't explain it."

They were on the off-ramp now, heading for home. The traffic was starting to thicken. It was after four in the afternoon. Rachel heard a car horn honking, but it was back on the freeway somewhere. At the end of the off-ramp they had to wait for a signal, one of those endless, ubiquitous lights. Rachel switched on the radio and pushed the tuning button, catching snatches of music, most of it rock or country. One station was playing "You Light Up My Life." The young singer belted out the refrains with a haunting, heart-tugging pathos that stirred Rachel's own pain, but she left it on anyway.

"Almost home," said Marlene, a surface brightness to her voice. Then, softly, "How's Brian taking all of this?"

The inquiry hit a vulnerable spot. Rachel winced in spite of herself. "Brian's terribly upset," she answered, turning down the radio. "He doesn't say much, but I know he doesn't understand what's happening. He never used to be close to his dad, really, but lately they were hitting it off well together. I have this feeling, Marlene, that Brian resents me now—maybe David and me both. I don't know."

"It's bound to be hard on him, Rachel."

"Well, what about me?" Rachel countered. It was as if a great torrent of outrage had suddenly burst upon her, spilling its juices over all the sane and proper emotions she thought were expected of her.

"What about me, anyway?" she repeated, her

voice shrill. "I have prayed for years, Marlene, you know that. For years I've prayed that David would come to Christ and that we'd finally have some unity in our family. For years I've gone to church alone and tried to bring up Brian in the church, in spite of his father's influence. Do you think David has ever for one moment bent my way? I kept on and took it all—the loneliness and the lack of communication—because I thought someday David would share my faith and things would be different. But now, now he's seeing some girl, some ditsy secretary from work. Maybe he's in love with her, I don't know. So what's left, Marlene? What's left of anything?"

"You said David wants to try again."

"Oh, I know," said Rachel, raking her fingers through her long, silken hair. She felt the futility tighten her lips. Anger was making her face feel unnatural, her very features distorted. She could only imagine what the bitterness was doing to her heart. "I know David said we could try again, but I can't see what good it would do. What's going to make things any better as long as he has feelings for that girl?"

"Doesn't it say in the Bible that if a woman has an unbelieving husband and he wishes to stay with her, she shouldn't make him go?" asked Marlene evenly. "Doesn't it say she should stay with him, Rachel?"

"I never read that," Rachel replied, frowning. "I never saw that passage anywhere as far as I can remember." She snapped off the radio with a decisive flick of the wrist, suddenly having no desire at all to hear the final verse of "You Light Up My Life."

Chapter Seven

"That's about it," David said with a note of finality. "That's how things stand between Rachel and me right now. Not too pretty, huh? I guess I've made a real mess of things."

Kit sat beside him in his sleek sports car, her fingers playing with the strap of her black leather purse. She was wearing a lime green crocheted sweater and stylish denim jeans. He watched her and felt the knot of guilt and frustration in his gut relax a bit. No matter how awful he felt, Kit had a way of picking up his spirits. She had a smooth, polished attractiveness, a certain subtle aura of worldliness about her, although she was only twenty-five. Kit was smaller and blonder than Rachel and wore more makeup—always a glossy, magazine sort of look to her face—but if David thought about it at all, he realized that Kit was probably no prettier than Rachel, who somehow managed to appear both natural and elegant without all the makeup.

David looked more closely at Kit. Her expression

was clouded. He couldn't read it. What was she thinking now that she knew the whole story?

"I'm sorry, David," she said at last. "I'm really sorry."

He had driven her up to Signal Hill to talk. It was one of the few places in Long Beach where there was still a semblance of privacy. The hill was a jutting protuberance of land laced with narrow, weaving roads, its landscape blemished by oil pumps and drilling rigs. The hill was considered by some to be a lovers' lane, and no doubt police cars patrolled the area periodically to encourage reluctant drivers on the road again.

David wasn't bothered by the hill's reputation, because here he could look out and see the dazzling lights of the Los Angeles basin spread out before him. For David, there was no real darkness in this place where all cities joined together to create one huge metropolis. In this place, this city of cities, there were only sweeping galaxies of lights, like an ocean of stars.

"I didn't tell you all of this for you to be sorry, Kit," he said, swinging his thoughts back to their conversation. "Listen, Kit," he said gently, "I'm not trying to cry on your shoulder. I just want to be straight with you. Let you know how things are with me."

"I understand, David, really I do."

He chuckled. "Really? Then you're doing better than I am."

Kit's voice was soft, tentative. "David, just one thing. I wonder..."

"Yeah?"

"Well, Rachel and the baby and all this—how does it...how is it going to affect us?"

"What do you mean?"

"I guess I mean, where do we go from here?"

"I honestly don't know," he said, shaking his head. "I never thought Rachel would give me my walking papers, just like that," he admitted, aware of the pained tone his voice could not hide. "Then again, I never thought I'd blurt out my feelings for you like I did. I just don't know what's going to happen now."

"We never planned for this to happen between us, David. It just did."

David stared out the window, the tendon along his jaw tightening. "I know, Kit. But the truth is, I really don't know what I should do. When I think about throwing my marriage away, I feel sick inside. I care about Rachel. Even when we lost that close feeling we once had, I never stopped caring. But it looks like Rachel's taken any decision about our marriage out of my hands. Now that she knows I have feelings for you, even though its only been really a friendship so far, she doesn't want anything to do with me."

"Then maybe you just have to accept that, David."

He looked back at Kit, his brow furrowed. "No matter what, I can't just walk away from her, Kit. Especially now, with a baby coming. I just can't get the idea of the baby out of my mind."

"You sound almost...happy about the baby."

"Happy? I suppose I am. I was shocked at first. Rachel and I never considered having another child. I've been so busy with work, and she's always leading a drama group at her church or taking classes for some degree she hopes to get someday. But it's my baby, as much a part of me as it is of her. It's just like when Brian was coming; I love the little tyke already, sight unseen. I don't want to be a part-time father to my child. Nor to Brian. He's a teenager. He needs me now, too."

"But what can you do if Rachel won't let you come home?"

He shrugged again, feeling suddenly tired and used up. He wished he could be asleep, dreaming of something that mattered to no one. "I honestly don't know," he said seriously. "The thing is," he continued, "I never started out to deceive Rachel or hurt her. And I don't want to hurt you, Kit. I don't even know how I stumbled into this whole thing. Somehow I've got to make Rachel understand that all I want is a decent life that makes some sense."

"Can you have that with Rachel? A happy, fulfilling life?"

David looked at Kit quickly, noting an edge of annoyance—even frustration—in her voice.

"I don't know if I can still have a happy life with Rachel or not. We've lived in our separate worlds for so long. But like I said, Rachel's so furious with me, it doesn't look like I'll get a chance to find out, does it?" he asked despondently.

An hour later David drove Kit home and waited patiently, mildly amused while she fished through her purse for her key. Kit carried a large purse and always had to fish for anything she wanted—a tissue, her compact, a dollar, whatever.

She found the key and looked up, smiling. "Can you come in a minute?" When he didn't answer, she said, "I could fix you some coffee or a sandwich. How about it?"

"Not tonight, Kit," he answered. "Your roommate probably needs her beauty sleep, and she'd have our heads if we woke her."

Kit flashed another kind of smile now and said with a softly alluring voice, "My roommate is in San Diego visiting friends, David. She won't be home until tomorrow afternoon."

For a brief moment David considered Kit's offer. A part of him argued, why not give in to your feelings? Where has being faithful got you? You've been kicked out of your own house. So much for fidelity!

But another part of him—a stronger part, a part that still held out hope of saving his marriage—resisted. "I'm sorry, Kit," he said, "I can't. I told Rachel you and I are not having an affair. I was glad I could tell her that." He sighed and looked into her eyes, aware of her peeved expression. "Kit, this whole thing—what we have—started out innocently enough, a simple office friendship. Maybe, in time, it could be something more." He drew in a sharp breath. "But I won't settle for a passing flirtation or just an affair."

"But David, if we truly care for each other, what's the harm?" Kit's voice took on a wheedling tone, a false note he'd never before noticed.

"I won't do that to Rachel, Kit. Nor to you. It's not fair to either of you. Nor to me. Don't you see? I don't want more confusion in my life. I want some answers, something with some meaning."

"Meaning? What meaning?"

He shrugged. "I don't know how to explain it, Kit. But there's this emptiness, like a gaping hole inside me, and I've got to fill it. But I don't know how. Rachel and I—well, it just seemed like we were at a dead end, an impasse. But now, with the baby coming, it's stirred up feelings I didn't know were still there. I just don't know what to do with them, Kit." He paused for a long time.

"I'm not trying to push you into anything, David," Kit whispered with a hurt tone.

He closed his eyes. "I—I know that, Kit," he said. "But I can't ask anything of you, and our relationship just can't go any further until I know I can make a real commitment. Until I know which way my life is going."

"All right, if that's the way it is, I understand," she murmured. "What you don't understand is that I'm not asking for any commitments, David."

He glanced over at her, but made no reply. He reached for the door handle and turned it. As the door swung open, he welcomed the inrush of brisk, head-clearing air. How could he admit to Kit that when they spoke of commitments, the only woman he could think about was Rachel?

Chapter Eight

In the weeks following her separation from her husband, Rachel found herself thinking frequently of the day she had spent with Marlene at Laguna Beach. Out of the wearisome accumulation of days since David had left, that day at Laguna stood alone as a sign that life could still be pleasant. She had to hold on to that idea—that life without David could be bearable.

Surprisingly, Rachel found herself thinking more and more in terms of *I* instead of *we*. *I* should take the car in for a tune-up. *I* must remember to send David's mother a birthday card. *I* must talk to Brian about his history grade.

She was a woman alone now and would have to assume the responsibilities of a woman alone. There was so much talk these days of what it meant to be a woman, of how she ought to fulfill herself as an individual. During her marriage, Rachel had not taken seriously the arguments and demands of the outspoken advocates of women's lib. After all, Rachel had known what her obligations were to David and Brian.

There had been no necessity to question her role as wife and mother.

In fact, if David had had his way, Rachel probably would have been a working mother instead of a stay-at-home mom pursuing occasional psychology and theater arts classes at the university. In the back of her mind Rachel had entertained the idea of getting a degree that would allow her to use drama therapy to counsel victims of abuse. But the closest she had come to achieving her goal was the drama group she led at church, where several troubled teenage girls had found a measure of emotional healing through their participation.

But even after all these years, Rachel was still a long way from being a qualified counselor. Perhaps she hadn't taken her studies seriously or hadn't truly believed she could achieve her goal. On another level, maybe she sensed that David would rather have her out earning a decent income at a real job instead of dabbling with her drama courses.

But all of that was beside the point now. It no longer mattered what David wanted. His wishes would no longer be her concern. She was on her own now.

But this new reality—this sudden, unexpected, unwanted freedom—raised brand-new, terrifying questions. What was her role now? What were her responsibilities? David was gone. Brian was growing up. Perhaps the time had come for Rachel to look after herself, to consider her own wishes and ambitions first for a change. Maybe after the baby came it would be time to get that degree. Carve out her own future.

Rachel browsed with greater interest through the

women's magazines at the supermarkets and drugstores. Every magazine seemed to contain articles proclaiming the rights of women. A woman's right to a career. Her right to divorce. Her right to have an abortion.

Her right to an abortion? This idea was especially foreign to Rachel. She was aware, of course, that millions of women had had abortions since the Supreme Court's Roe versus Wade decision over two decades ago. These days any woman could have an abortion for any reason, if she chose. Abortion on demand, they called it.

But Rachel hadn't seriously thought about abortion before, not personally. Not in the intimate way that a woman actually considers ending her unborn child's life.

She had always considered abortion wrong, a sin, even murder. Wouldn't it be murder in the eyes of God? Her pastor believed so. So did she, of course, though lately Rachel wasn't attending church as regularly as before, and might have dropped out altogether were it not for Brian, Marlene and her drama group.

Now that she was alone, she wasn't especially interested in what her pastor had to say. She felt that his sermons were hardly relevant to her painful situation. And she couldn't ignore the fact that she and David had started growing apart after she began attending services. David had never seen a need for religion and had resented her involvement in the church. Maybe he was right after all.

The truth was, Rachel didn't see where God was offering her a bit of help now that she was on her own. Her prayers, as infrequent as they were, had become vain repetitions, hardly profitable.

Rachel honestly dreaded the thought of raising a child alone. What kind of life could she give a child now? He would be virtually fatherless. Faced with the necessity to work, she would have little time to devote to an infant. The possibility of ending the helpless new life inside her was unthinkable to Rachel—even repugnant. Yet she felt so alone, so scared. How could she voice her secret questions and misgivings—and to whom?

Marlene, of course.

One afternoon Rachel dared to approach her with her questions and fears. She drew her words carefully, anticipating Marlene's sympathy and support. But she was hardly ready for Marlene's impassioned response.

"Rachel, honey, you're facing the toughest moment of your life right now. Anyone would be terrified. But you're going to be all right," she assured her. "Children are a blessing of God. Why, I'd love to have a sweet little baby of my own."

"I wish it were you and not me," Rachel said despondently.

Marlene shook her head, a wistful smile playing on her lips. "I haven't done more than shake hands with a man in five years, so no babies for me, unless God wants to try a repeat performance of His best miracle."

"I don't know, Marlene. I'm just so scared. I just can't see myself raising a baby alone. It was hard enough raising Brian even with David's help."

Marlene squeezed Rachel's hand. "God will give you the grace, honey. Just trust in Him."

Rachel slumped home, her intentions unresolved. The agony of indecision tore at her mind.

Marlene saw everything in terms of black and white, and, what's more, she seemed to have no trouble determining what was black and what was white. *If only I could see things with equal clarity,* Rachel lamented. .

When David stopped by to pick up Brian for a football game one Saturday afternoon, Rachel again—inadvertently—stumbled onto the subject of abortion. David had asked how she was feeling and made some comment about the baby's birth. When Rachel appeared hesitant, David pressed her for information.

"Is something wrong, Rae?" he inquired, following her into the kitchen. "Is there some problem with your pregnancy?"

Rachel poured two cups of coffee and handed him one.

"Did you hear me, Rae?" he demanded. "You are healthy, aren't you? You've seen the doctor and everything's on course, right?"

She sipped her coffee, flustered, and groped for words. "Yes, everything's okay. It's just—I've been thinking a lot about the baby."

"Well, believe me, so have I." David set his coffee cup on the table and reached out and touched her arm, lightly, tentatively, as if he weren't sure he still had a right to touch her. "And I'm going to be here for you, Rachel. Whatever you need, you let me know, okay?"

Tears stung her eyes. "But I—I'm so scared. I don't know if I really want this baby," she admitted.

David stared incredulously at her. "What are you

saying? Of course you want the baby. It's a done deal.'' He sucked in a breath and his eyes narrowed. ''Wait a minute. Are you saying...you're not thinking about an abortion, are you?'' Without waiting for her reply David slammed his open palm down hard on the table, jarring his coffee cup. ''You've got to be kidding!''

Rachel knew she'd never do such a thing, but she resented his attitude. What right did he have to tell her what to do after he'd left her to face this all alone?

''It's not up to you,'' she said defensively.

David's voice softened. ''Not you, Rachel. You wouldn't do such a thing. I know you too well.''

Rachel felt herself wavering. ''No, I could never,'' she admitted. ''It's just hard to face this...alone.''

He stepped toward her and gently caressed her shoulder. ''Rae, you're not alone. It's my baby, too.''

Tears pooled in her eyes. ''How could I forget that?''

He clasped both her arms and stared at her with an intensity she hadn't seen in ages. ''Maybe you think I don't care about this baby, Rachel? Is that it? You think I'm deserting my family? Well, let me remind you. You're the one who sent me packing. I never said I wanted out of this marriage. I never said I didn't want our baby.''

She bit her lower lip to hold back a sob. ''You didn't have to say those things, David. You said something worse. You said you might love someone else. Do you honestly think we can hold together our marriage or our family without love? How can we bring a baby into a home without love?''

''I shouldn't have said that, Rachel. I don't know what I feel anymore. I just—''

"Are you still seeing her?"

"Who? Kit? Yes, I've seen her, but—"

"Then we have nothing else to talk about."

His grip tightened on her arms. "That's just it. We haven't talked anything out since this whole mess began. But if you think I'm going to let you abort my baby—"

"Your baby? You're a fine one to talk about your baby!"

He drew her against him with unexpected tenderness. "I love that baby, Rachel. Sight unseen. It's my baby, and I love it already."

Perhaps she loved the baby, too. *Dear God, I hope so,* she prayed. Perhaps after she stopped feeling so sorry for herself and so afraid, she'd even look forward to this baby's birth. If only things were the way they'd been before Brian's birth.

She felt the nubby fabric of David's sports jacket against her cheek and felt herself grow weak in his arms. "Oh, David, why did you have to spoil everything?"

He spoke out of a raw anguish. "I didn't mean to, Rae, I swear!"

Tears spilled down her cheeks. Suddenly she wanted nothing more than to remain in her husband's arms and let him comfort her. His closeness was more than she could endure. The scent of his aftershave, the minty warmth of his breath, the warm, solid feeling of him sent shock waves through her system. She wanted him back—how she wanted him. But she couldn't accept charity, or David's pity. He was in love with someone else now. She refused to take the crumbs of affection he tossed her. She stiffened and disengaged herself from his arms. Coolly she said,

"I'll get through this somehow, I guess. You don't have to worry about me."

Before he could answer, Brian came bounding into the room, greeting his father with a loud, "Hey, Dad, I'm just about ready. It should be a great game, huh?"

A look of confusion, anger and regret crossed David's face, but with Brian in the room, their conversation had come to an abrupt halt. With a hapless gesture of frustration, David turned to his son and rumpled his hair. "Hey, big guy, you look like you've grown another foot since I saw you last."

"I have, Dad." Brian laughed. "Hey, with three feet I should make the soccer team—easy!"

"Three feet? Yeah, I getcha!"

While David's attention was diverted to Brian, Rachel slipped soundlessly to her bedroom and locked the door after her. She collapsed on the empty king-size bed and stared up at the ceiling. "Dear God, what am I going to do? What am I going to do!"

Rachel felt like crying, but the tears wouldn't come. A phrase was pounding over and over in her mind—"Wait on the Lord. Be of good courage." The words stayed with her.

Finally she began to cry. "God forgive me for not wanting this child," Rachel whispered again and again. "I do not want this baby. Forgive me!"

Chapter Nine

Brian Webber stood in a casual slouch, craning his neck as he studied his reflection in the bathroom mirror. When he jutted out his lower lip in a disdainful sneer, he figured he looked like a young James Dean. Real young. Or maybe he was just seeing what he wanted to see. He slipped his comb from his jeans pocket and tossed back his straight, light brown hair. He had a system for combing his hair, starting from his forehead and working his way back along each side. Of course, ten minutes after he combed it, it would be hanging in his face again. But why sweat it? He was in a good mood. He was stoked.

"Hey, dude, I got four days off from school," he said aloud. "Man, those Thanksgiving holidays! No worries! Just kickin' it!" Of course, two days were the regular weekend he'd have anyway, but the four days together made more than half a week. "Man, you can do a whole lot with more than half a week."

The first three months of eighth grade were behind him. It was no big thing anymore being in eighth grade. He was settled into the dreary routine of classes and cafeteria lunches and more classes and only now and then a school assembly to break the monotony of it all. He was looking forward to ninth grade, the first year of high school. Reaching a goal like that might make the tedium bearable. Being in high school was a lot better than saying, "I'm in the eighth grade."

Brian's friend, Ronnie Mayhew, was in the ninth grade, and he let you know it. He waved it around like a flag, his being a *freshman.* Actually, Ronnie was fifteen and should have been in tenth grade, but he had flunked a grade somewhere back in elementary school. He didn't like to say much about it, and Brian, not wanting to cross Ronnie, never brought the subject up.

This past year had been a mystery to Brian. Until this year he had not thought much about who he was or what he was doing. Certain things were expected of him and he did them. He had never had to weigh his actions against other possible actions. He did what he was told by his parents, his instructors and Sunday school teachers. He was a good kid—everyone said so. Not until this year had he considered that he might not be good, that there might be other choices open to him.

It was an electrifying thought to a vulnerable, questioning teen. When he thought about the choices opening up to him he felt giddy inside, possessed of some strange new power—the ability to choose for himself. He kept these thoughts private, churning them over and over in his mind, savoring them like pieces of mouthwatering candy.

However, such delicious thoughts of power and

choice always managed to melt away as Brian was pulled back into the routine of the day, the regimen of history lessons, English assignments, book reports and outside reading. There was the photography club after school on Tuesdays, and he was on the track team. When he hadn't made the soccer squad, the coach had said, "You're a fast runner, Webber. Try out for track." Now he was one of his school's fastest runners, but it still wasn't soccer.

If Brian had to pinpoint his favorite pastime, it was surfing the Internet. Man, that World Wide Web was out of sight. He could spend a lifetime in cyberspace, cruising from chat room to chat room, connecting with strangers all over the world. There was an exhilarating power in knowing that with a few clicks of the mouse you could be talking up a storm with some guy in Nairobi or some girl in Bogota or Berlin. Brian usually said he was nineteen and in college—surely a harmless lie. After all, who would want to talk seriously with a guy just thirteen?

Besides school, sports and the Internet, Brian had church. He was chairman of his Sunday school class, although he had no idea what the title meant or what was expected of him in that position. He was also on the social committee for his youth group, planning Friday-night activities—bowling, pizza parties, video nights, or beach trips. He got a kick out of arranging things; he liked taking charge. "Have Brian do it. He'll take care of everything," the other kids would say. He liked that.

Brian considered himself a Christian. He had no doubt about certain things. Jesus, for one. Jesus was in him, and Jesus was God Himself. Until recently, there were times when Brian could almost feel the power of Jesus welling up inside him. Nothing was impossible for him with Jesus as his best friend. Yes, the two of them together had been an unbeatable combination.

But lately, things had blurred, out of focus, and Brian's ideas of Jesus got mixed up with his image of Mr. Lipton, his Sunday school teacher, a timorous little man who wore wire-rim spectacles and red suspenders and rarely understood the language of eighth graders. Brian felt sorry for Mr. Lipton and would dutifully sit still during his lessons, perhaps to make up for the restlessness, the whispers and shuffling of feet of the other guys in class. But Brian resented having to sit so still when he was anxious to get up and go do something. He wished Mr. Lipton would wise up and quit teaching Sunday school and go take up the collection or something.

Once Brian had had a really cool Sunday school teacher, Ray Johnson, who was twenty-three and had played football in college. Ray always had something to say that made his students think. Brian learned it was fun to think past the surface grooves everybody usually fell into. It was Ray who got Brian to pray out loud in class and memorize Scripture. But then last year Ray Johnson married his college sweetheart and took a job in Ohio, so now probably another bunch of kids somewhere in Cleveland were getting the benefit of Ray Johnson.

Thinking about it now, it seemed to Brian that it had been years since Ray Johnson was part of his life. Maybe because so many of Brian's feelings and attitudes had changed this past year. He was back to that. Back to this new confusion, this new ecstasy of choices. Who did he really have to be responsible to?

Himself? He hardly knew yet what he wanted from himself. Responsible to his parents? Them?

Who were they anymore? Who? They didn't even live together now. They were *separated.* Maybe they would get a divorce. Half the kids Brian knew had divorced parents. There was always a raw, defensive edge to them, kids with divorced parents—as if they were being secretly pulled in several directions at once and had learned to be suspicious of anything the world had to offer.

Brian had never expected to be one of those kids. He had always pitied them, because they were helpless to change anything. There was no way they could pull things together and make their families work. No way they could put the broken pieces together. It was as if they were hanging in a chasm between two sheer cliffs, suspended between two unmoving forces, and no matter what they did they couldn't save themselves. There was nowhere to go but down. Splat! You're dead. Brian hated to think of being so helpless, so lost. It wasn't fair, and he wanted no part of anything unfair.

But now, whether he liked it or not, Brian was like those other kids, helpless and wide-eyed and raw with emotions he had never expected to feel. He hated it. No one had asked him what he wanted. No one cared how he felt. His family had been split in two and his folks acted as if he wasn't even involved, as if it was just their problem and he had no choice but to go along for the ride. Bumpy at best. Harrowing for sure.

Brian loved his folks, both of them, in different ways. But he also hated them, although he realized this was a sin. He'd hated them most of all the night his dad left. Why did he leave all of a sudden, without warning, with no hint at all to prepare Brian for this sudden hurt?

And what about his mother, who loved Jesus just as Brian did—why hadn't she loved his father enough to stop him? Adults were weird people who rarely did things the way you'd expect. They demanded so much more from things, from people. They had a way of making life more complicated than it needed to be.

Brian hated feeling so confused about his parents and his own affections and loyalties. Most of his life he had been closer to his mother than to his father. He and his mother went to church together and even used to pray together at bedtime, until he'd protested, announcing he was too old for such kiddie rituals. He felt bad about hurting her feelings, but what was a guy to do? Still, from the time he was a kid, he'd sensed he was right to go his mother's way.

His father was a totally cool guy who kept things to himself, who said little or nothing, and because Brian didn't know his father well, he feared him a little. His dad never went with them to church, and religion wasn't discussed in his presence. God belonged to Brian and his mother, and to bring up the subject of God to his father would have been awkward for all of them. A few times his father had dressed up in his best suit and gone with them to church—to a Christmas play or the Bible school children's program or an Easter cantata. Brian was always overwhelmingly proud of his father during these occasions. After all, some of the kids doubted Brian even had a father. "You mean, you got a dad? I never saw him, not in two years," someone had said to him once. Brian never forgot.

I have a totally rad father, he wanted the world to

know. And now that he was older, Brian understood his father better—or had until his dad walked out. And even now he envied him his power to do what he pleased. In spite of everything, Brian felt a new camaraderie with his father. They were men and shared a man's power and love of freedom. It was a mystery, this power of men, which Brian was anxious to unravel and claim for himself.

Someday Brian would be free to come and go like his father. He would be his own boss. He would have a man's freedom.

Over the years Brian had wondered what his dad did during those free hours while his wife and son were at church. What did he do with so much free time and all the rooms of the house to himself? Brian knew his dad slept late on Sunday mornings, and sometimes when they got home at noon, his father was still sitting at the breakfast table drinking a cup of black coffee and reading the Sunday paper. What was this private world of his dad's like—that he had to answer to no one, not to Brian, not to Brian's mother, apparently not even to God?

Brian's mother was easier to understand. She had always put God and the church first, and Brian and his father before herself. It was that simple. Brian could always count on her to do whatever was *right.* Right was an indispensable word to his mother. Right had priority over everything else, even over a person's own desire for something. There were times when Brian wished he could tell his mother to do what *she* wanted to do for a change—it would have been better, he thought, than having her do something only because it was the "right" thing to do. But these instances were vague in his mind, and if at times his mother was resentful of something, it wasn't a reality he could grasp or cope with. So he left it alone.

In fact, now that he was growing up, his parents were no longer his primary interest. And now that they were flying off crazily in opposite directions, he couldn't think of them without feeling a little sick inside.

Now it seemed terribly important to win the respect and admiration of someone like Ronnie Mayhew, a ninth grader already wise to the world. There was a quality of intoxication about Ronnie, a swaggering confidence that held Brian spellbound. He was hypnotized by Ronnie's worldliness, by his apparent ability to cope with anything life threw at him. In contrast, Brian felt painfully vulnerable, a weakness he tried feverishly to hide from every living soul. No one must know how unsure he was of himself, how easily he could be hurt by people. If it were possible, he would gladly confiscate all the boldness and self-confidence Ronnie possessed.

The next best thing was to hang around Ronnie long enough for his self-confidence to rub off on Brian. That's why he had chosen Ronnie Mayhew to be his best friend.

From the first, Brian had been awed by Ronnie's swaggering manner; his shaved head and the ring in his left ear added to the allure. Ronnie was barely passing in school and teased Brian for worrying so much about getting good grades.

It was rumored around that Ronnie drank liquor, maybe even worse. No one knew for sure, but that's what was said. Brian felt uneasy about the rumors. Ronnie rarely brought up the subject, and Brian had no desire to discuss it either, since using alcohol or drugs, according to his mom, was one of the really gross sins, and totally dangerous.

While Ronnie didn't say much about it, he did bring up the subject of shoplifting, describing it as one of his more entertaining pastimes. A guy who was real cool could shoplift and never get caught, he said. A guy who lost his cool—or who wasn't willing to try in the first place—was a mama's brat, a real loser, a first-class dork.

Ronnie dazzled Brian with his tales of going into department and discount stores and lifting CDs, cameras, video games, pagers, even car CD players, right in front of smart-mouthed clerks who never saw a thing. He was sly, Ronnie was. Brian had no idea what was truth and what was fiction. It hardly mattered as long as Ronnie boasted so convincingly of his escapades. To Brian's mind, it took nerve just to make such daring claims.

Brian had none of Ronnie's reckless courage; he had only a wistful longing to be Ronnie's equal. Listening to Ronnie, vicariously living his experiences, Brian inevitably came up short by comparison. He could think of nothing significant or memorable about himself. What could he do? How could he ever possess the steely-jawed guts of a Ronnie Mayhew?

With these thoughts in mind, coupled with immense self-doubt, Brian Webber resolved to make his first serious attempt at shoplifting. He imagined telling Ronnie about if afterward and showing off the loot he'd swiped, maybe even giving Ronnie some of it. After giving the matter a great deal of thought, Brian chose the Friday after Thanksgiving Day as the time to prove himself. On Thanksgiving Eve, lying on his back on his rumpled bed, his hands cupped under his head, Brian pondered what type of store to try—department store, discount, music, electronics? Large or small? How did a guy determine such a thing? Finally, swinging his legs over the side of the bed, he decided a local discount store would be his first target.

On Thanksgiving Day, alone with his mother, Brian was silent, locked into his secret thoughts. His emotions swung back and forth like a pendulum. He was at first enthralled and then appalled by the prospects of the coming day. Was it really in him to break the law, to commit such a crime, a sin? Would Jesus forgive him? Would He? But Brian could hardly ask forgiveness yet—when he hadn't even done the evil deed. Would God forgive him later?

He considered praying, but Ronnie Mayhew was closer to him now than God. He even thought of talking to his parents, but who were they now, and where were they really? They were at separate poles, each flying out forever into some distant region beyond him. Unreachable. They would never come back, though his mother was with him every day and he saw his father on weekends. They were gone, both of them, inexplicably, absolutely gone.

In a calm, perfunctory fashion, Brian dressed and ate his breakfast on Friday morning. Juice, toast, corn flakes and a banana. He wasn't a bit nervous; no sir, he was in perfect control. When his mother asked him where he was going, he said quickly, "Nowhere. Just out."

She wouldn't let it rest. "Aren't you going with the youth group to the beach?"

He'd forgotten about the beach party. "No, not this time."

"But you always go."

"It's boring."

"Since when? You love the beach."

No use arguing. "Maybe I'll catch a ride later with one of the guys." Before his mother could reply, he surprised her with a hint of a kiss on her smooth cheek. Then he was out the door—fast! Without looking back, he climbed on his bike and rode away into the cool, smudged California sunlight. He parked his bike in the rack on the sidewalk several yards from the discount store. Usually he'd lock his bike, but decided not to this time.

He entered the store in quick, nervous strides, his hands jammed into his jacket pockets, his eyes darting from counter to counter. He was a guy with a purpose. Inside the store, towering aisles of merchandise stretched from wall to wall, forever. Amid the maze of gleaming counters and beckoning products was the hustle of people with shopping carts and packages and small children, the low hum of voices and the savory aromas of popcorn and baked goods. Brian passed the long row of checkout stands and made his way through housewares. His eye roved critically over the dishes, pots and pans, utensils and crazy stuff women found ways of using in their kitchens. Obviously there was nothing here for him.

In addition to the usual hum of activity inside the store, Brian became aware of another hum, high-pitched and intense, in his own head. It seemed to increase as he padded in his sneakers down one aisle and up another. He sauntered through men's wear to the music department and stopped to read the list of the top ten songs on the chart. He licked his dry lips as he browsed through some of the higher-priced

CDs. They might work. He had made a hole in his jacket pocket so that when he took something it would drop through the hole into the lining. He could hold several small items that way—a camera, a calculator, a wallet, a watch, surely a CD. But he had to be careful. Very careful. He couldn't look suspicious, as if he was loitering or up to no good.

He drifted back to men's wear, hoping he had the purposeful walk of a customer about to make a purchase. Take your time, take it easy, he told himself, forcing his thoughts against the incessant hum in his head. The hum was becoming a pressure. He could feel sweat gathering like mad at the back of his neck and in his armpits. Next thing, it'd be running down his arms. What was he doing? Was he going crazy, walking around looking for something to steal?

He examined a small leather case with nail clippers, a file and other gadgets attached to a red velvet insert. His dad could use something like that. He turned it over in his hand, feeling the leather. The price tag said $10.95.

"May I help you, young man?" asked the clerk, a pale little man in a gray suit, a bright red tie his only distinguishing feature. The tie overpowered him—even Brian could see that. The little man was all red tie.

"No, sir," Brian said, releasing the leather case as if it had caught fire. "I'm just looking, just looking for something for my dad, sir."

Brian walked away, forcing himself to pace his steps. Don't look as if you're running; don't look suspicious, you big dope!

He would have to do something fast. His nerves were jumping out of his skin. Sweat was beading on his forehead and upper lip. His face felt weird, flushed and chilly at once. It was now or never—do it or forget it. He returned to the music department and riffled through the CDs. They were out in the open on a cardboard display on the counter. Brian read the titles, wondering which one he should take. The Supertones or the Mighty Mighty Bosstones—two popular ska bands? Or MxPx, a rad punk band, Ronnie's favorite?

The pressure in Brian's skull was increasing. He could imagine two strong hands squeezing the soft jelly substance of his brain, crushing his thoughts and plans, twisting his reason. What was the matter with him? What kind of dumb, scared chicken was he, anyway?

He selected a CD—The Supertones—and attempted to slam the square plastic cartridge into his jacket pocket. He fumbled, snagging a corner of the CD on the inside lining of his pocket. The CD careened to the tile floor, making a sharp *thwack* as it hit. Embarrassed, flustered, Brian knelt to retrieve the item, bringing it swiftly back to its place on the counter.

He looked up into the face of a clerk, a thick, stern-faced woman with flaring nostrils and sagging jowls, who stared back at him from behind dark-rimmed, suspicious spectacles. She knew—guessed—everything! Brian was sure of it, just as he was sure that at this very moment he might strangle and die at her feet.

"You want to buy it?" she said, dripping sarcasm.

Brian's body was withering, shriveling up, under the woman's critical gaze. She remained imperturbable, watching him.

"No, thanks," he croaked as flames of embarrassment crept up his face. Surely the clerk had X-ray vision and could read his very thoughts. Brian turned on his heel and sprinted toward the exit door. No looking back, not once. Straight out, man, away, before a security guard grabs your shoulder!

He hopped on his bike and pedaled swiftly home, breathless, shaken and dazed. The sum total of his senses had been shredded into crazy little fragments, like torn paper, blowing away, scattered everywhere. He couldn't trust himself, didn't know what to do with himself.

When he got home he went straight to the bathroom and vomited. His mother stood outside the door, demanding, "Do you have the flu, sweetheart? Do you want me to take your temperature?"

When she saw his chalky white face, she sent him straight to bed, brought him a cup of broth and force-fed him some nasty pink medicine. As she hung up his rumpled jacket, she said, "You're much too sick to spend Thanksgiving weekend with your father, dear. You're staying home in bed."

Brian groaned. So much for the fantastic holiday he had dreamed of for months. So much for his fleeting life of crime! And like a sign from heaven, the next time he put on his brown leather jacket, he found that the hole in the pocket had been mysteriously sewn up.

Chapter Ten

Rachel could not decide about the tree, whether the lights should be all one color, or whether she should use a variety of colors. It was not a real tree this year. She felt a little bad about that, but real trees were so expensive. And a real tree would have implied something—a real celebration, an actual family get-together, which this was not. Christmas would be just like Thanksgiving—no big family dinner with turkey and dressing, just chicken in the broiler and a deli salad. It would be Rachel and Brian together, formal and vaguely restless, doing random things and wondering where the meaning was.

It shouldn't be this way, she thought. I should do something about it. I should do something. She sat down on the sofa and stared at the small artificial tree she had purchased that afternoon. It was silver; even the base had been sprayed with silver paint, and there were places on the sides of the base where the paint was splotchy and dull wood showed through.

In the store the tree hadn't looked half bad. It was

bright and glittery; it fit in with all the tinsel and baubles crowding the store counters. There was artificial snow on the counters—thick sparkling stuff that was warm to the touch. The little silver tree had been sitting there in the warm snow, and she had picked up the tree, brandishing it before the other shoppers like some sort of special promise. She had gone straight to the checkout stand, trying to keep this new feeling of satisfaction from dissolving. But the feeling was gone before she reached home.

Now, looking at the tree, Rachel had an impulse to laugh. The tree was funny, a regular riot. Hilarious. What kind of tree was this, anyway? It would get the gold lights, which it deserved—the ones that showed tarnished places. The bad spots would look like reflections, dark and a little muddled. No one would look close enough to see the bad places.

That decided, Rachel got up and walked across the room to inspect the tree from another angle. It looked the same, a simple matter of wires and cellophane and tinfoil or something. She should have bought a regular tree with the scent of fresh pine needles, a real one that made the place look like Christmas. That's what she needed—a real tree.

She had been willing to go out to one of those lots where trees stood in great bunches, their branches lush, sweet and prickly. She was willing. She would have gone even to the mountains—to Big Bear, perhaps—where they might have been able to cut down their own tree. Rachel was willing to do this and more, all for the sake of a tree, for the sake of Christmas. But Brian couldn't care less. Brian, who loved Christmas, had said, "I don't care what you do. Do whatever you want. I don't have time to go running around looking for a tree.''

So Rachel didn't care, either—couldn't afford to care. The silver tree would do nicely. It was adequate. Perhaps it was better than the tree David had this year, if he had bothered with one. She hoped he had. He needed something, a tree at least. It would be a ragged sort of bond between them—their own private, separate trees, just adequate.

Or had David gone all out and had a really magnificent tree? Had he invited her—that girl—to decorate it for him? She pictured them sitting cozily together on a couch, admiring their handiwork together, the lights low, David's arm slung comfortably around the girl's shoulders. What would they do? What would they do Christmas Day?

Whenever David came to see Brian, to pick him up and drive him off somewhere, he rarely said anything important to Rachel. His conversation was just so many words, small talk, little necessary connections linking this action to that. It was like a chain, a series of steps, everything in logical order: David in the doorway greeting her; David looking at his watch, hurrying Brian along; David flashing that opaque smile that kept his thoughts private and mysterious; David and Brian going out the door, the door shutting and the sequence over, ended just like that.

This was Christmas Eve and David might drop by. He might drop by tomorrow, Christmas. There would be the brief, meaningless blocks of conversation between them, the overdone politeness, but it would be better than this silence in the walls. It would be better with David here, but that was something she shouldn't think about. It was dangerous thinking like that.

Rachel stared coolly at the tree, staring it down, ridiculing it, reminding herself that she did not want a husband in the house who did not love her. She was better off without him. She would get better. Would God expect her to stay with a man who... Marlene said yes. Marlene said God would certainly want her to...

"For crying out loud, let's get some lights on this tree," Rachel said aloud. Her voice came back at her like wind; she sounded a little crazy talking to herself like that.

If only somebody would come over. Marlene had said she might stop by—she had a few gifts to bring over. She might be here at any time, any minute.

If only Brian were home—even Brian, who kept her at a distance now and never said words that meant anything. He was getting just like his father, closed up and involved in things that had nothing to do with her.

Rachel didn't really worry about Brian; he was a good boy. He was growing up. It was part of growing up to grow away from people. It was to be expected. Sometimes Rachel would try to imagine what Brian was doing when he was not at home or in school. Often when he walked in the door, she would say, "What did you do today, Brian?" He would grunt or scowl as if she had said something stupid.

She would ask him again, patiently, as if saying the words for the first time. "I was over at Ronnie's," he would reply. If she pursued the subject he would say, "We were listening to CDs," or "We were surfing the Internet," or "We just kicked it." She would nod uncertainly, wondering what she could do to open him up. Why did she let him get away with such evasive answers? Why didn't she make him talk, tell her something? Why didn't she? Maybe because of her own guilt, nameless and persistent. That was probably it. Yes.

The doorbell rang and Rachel answered it quickly, expectantly. This was Christmas Eve! Someone was here to see her. This was a time to be merry.

"Merry Christmas, Rachel, honey!"

It was Marlene. She had too many presents in her arms and was dropping them. Like an inept juggler, she was trying hard to balance all the gifts in her arms at once. "Oh, I should have made two trips," she said.

"Come on in, don't just stand in the doorway," said Rachel, moving aside, offering her arms for some of the gifts. "Marlene, you shouldn't have. I don't even have all of yours wrapped."

"Doesn't matter. I just tear the wrapping off, anyway. These are all for you and Brian and the baby, believe it or not. I found all these little things I wanted to get, so I did, instead of one big thing. The most fun is having lots of little packages."

"That's the truth," said Rachel, carefully placing the gifts on the sofa. She glanced at her little silver tree, still not decorated. "I haven't got the tree finished yet. We'll just put these here for now."

"Where did you get your tree?" Marlene sounded dubious.

"Kmart. This afternoon. I decided not to fuss with a real one."

"Well, I should have thought of something like that," said Marlene agreeably. She fussed with her packages, arranging them carefully on the sofa. "These are for Brian," she said, nodding at one stack of gifts. She looked around. "Where is Brian?"

"He's supposed to be home, but you know kids. Always off somewhere else, anywhere but home."

"But it's Christmas Eve."

"I know. He's over at his friend's. Ronnie Mayhew. I told him to get home before dark."

"He's been over there quite a bit lately, hasn't he?" Marlene noted. "He's something else, isn't he? What do you think of that boy, Rachel?"

"Ronnie Mayhew? I can't say I like him. He's strange. Looks like a skinhead, but then lots of boys have shaved heads these days. It doesn't have to mean anything. He acts polite enough around me, but I'm sure that's just a facade. I have no idea what he's really like."

"But Brian likes him?"

"Oh, yes. He's needed a good friend since David moved out. You should see it. Brian adores Ronnie, follows him around like a little puppy dog. Brian is sold on him."

"I suppose that's the important thing," said Marlene doubtfully.

"I suppose," Rachel agreed. "But I'm just as glad they don't spend too much time here. That boy gives me the creeps."

Marlene sat down on the velvet sofa and fussed again with one of the packages, straightening a bow, fluffing it gently. She was wearing black polyester pants and an oversize sweatshirt with Merry Christmas written in red and green puffy paint. "Maybe I shouldn't ask this—just say so—" she said, "but is Brian going to see his dad this Christmas?"

"Sure, Marlene." Rachel sat down in the old recliner that had been David's favorite. "Of course Brian will see his father. It wouldn't be Christmas otherwise, would it?" Rachel felt her face grow warm. Her cheeks were probably red; Marlene would see that she was flustered. She laughed, sounding nervous, even to herself. "You know Brian will spend part of Christmas with David. I don't want to break up those two. Don't worry, they have their times together."

Marlene's voice grew confidential. "How is David, do you know?"

Rachel sighed involuntarily. "Oh, he's doing all right. I guess he's worried about his job. You know how things are in aerospace lately. Another of their periodic slumps. David says the whole industry could go right down the tubes. He says a lot of good guys have been laid off. They're out pounding the pavement, looking for work."

"Does he think he might be next?"

"He didn't say that, but I suppose it's on his mind."

Marlene frowned, but her expression softened as she said, "I want you to know, Rachel. I'm praying for you and David. I still believe things will work out for you two. I just know it."

Rachel nodded without conviction, and smiled. Her smile felt pasted on, not quite there. "I'm afraid that's just wishful thinking, Marlene."

They were both silent a moment until Marlene tried another subject. "How have you been feeling, Rachel?"

Rachel's hands went instinctively to her middle. "Not bad. I'm finally over the morning sickness, thank goodness! For a while I didn't think I'd make it."

"You did look pretty green around the gills for a while."

"Green is an understatement! I even had to have Betty McCutcheon take over the drama group at church. At least until after the baby comes."

Marlene nodded. "Betty's good. She did little theater for years, didn't she?"

"Yes, and she's already scheduled our group for several drug-abuse-prevention assemblies and a battered wives' shelter."

"Terrific. That's what the group does best, right? What do you call it? Therapeutic drama?"

Rachel nodded. "That's what Betty's so good at. I envy her. She's working toward her degree in marriage, family and child counseling, you know."

"That's the degree you should be trying for."

"Don't I wish! But it's awfully ironic, isn't it? Thinking of counseling troubled marriages? Sort of like the blind trying to heal the blind?"

"Well, it takes one to know one. Think of how much empathy you'll have. You could do it, Rachel. You've taken lots of courses. You must be over halfway to your degree by now."

"Yes, I am. And maybe I will complete it someday—when the baby's in college." Rachel flashed a sardonic smile. "But I'm afraid I haven't seen many counselors going around with gray hair, geriatric shoes and a walker."

"It won't take you that long to get your degree, honey, not once you set your mind to it."

"I suppose I could wear the baby to classes like a papoose."

"Now you're talking." They lapsed into silence again. Then Marlene said, "You're starting to show, Rachel. That's good. Have you started wearing maternity clothes yet?"

"No. I don't go out all that much. Especially now that I'm not directing the drama group. I've become a regular couch potato. I have all these old shirts of David's. They're comfortable, so I wear them—just around the house, of course."

"You look good," said Marlene. "Better than you have in weeks."

Rachel paused. "I've been feeling pretty good. In fact, I'm surprised I feel so good. Sometimes I don't even feel pregnant." She wondered if she should go on with her thoughts. Might as well—Marlene might as well know how she felt. "You know, Marlene," she said quietly, "sometimes I go for days hardly thinking about the baby. Is that normal?"

Marlene's expression darkened. "I don't know, hon. I've never been a mother. Never even close."

Rachel's voice quivered; she tried to steady it. "The baby—it still doesn't mean anything to me, Marlene. I don't think about the baby, and I know it's not right, but sometimes I still don't want it."

Marlene sat up, surprise and dismay registering in her eyes. "Rachel, honey, I thought it was all settled. I know you won't regret keeping your baby. Wait till he starts kicking and you know he's there. You'll just fall crazy in love with him."

"I'm sure you're right," said Rachel, looking faintly distracted. "But without David here to share the pregnancy with me...I don't know. Sometimes even Brian acts like he's embarrassed by my condition."

A sound outside the door drew their attention—a scuffing of feet, a sharp clicking noise. The door flew open and Brian came bursting inside, his face flushed with something like merriment or wonder. His eyes glistened, almost a glazed sheen, perhaps from the wind. He grinned, showing the line of milky white teeth. "Hi, Marlene, hi, Mom," he said, unbuttoning his hooded canvas parka. He sounded cheerier than he had in days. "Merry Christmas. It won't be long now!"

"How come you're so late, Brian?" Rachel asked, her words separate and concise. "What were you doing all this time?"

"Oh, Mom," he whined, sounding suddenly like an exasperated old man. "I was at Ronnie's, Mom. I told you where I was going."

"But I told you to be home before dark. What were you doing?"

"Chillin', Mom. We were just chillin', that's all." Brian gave an abrupt nod as if to excuse himself and strode straight to his room, closing the door noisily behind him.

Rachel looked at Marlene and shook her head in exasperation. "That boy! Sometimes I don't know what to think."

Marlene offered a warmly sympathetic smile. "It has to be hard on him, his parents separated, especially at Christmas."

Rachel averted her gaze. She didn't want to get into this with Marlene again. She would only end up feeling angry and resentful. Marlene had a way of making her feel as if their separation was her fault as much as David's, but it wasn't true. Rachel was the injured party in this mess. David was the one who'd gone looking for greener pastures. So was Rachel wrong to hope David found himself knee-deep in cow chips?

The doorbell sounded again, an insistent ring. Marlene stood. "I'd better go. Looks like you've got more company."

"No, don't go," said Rachel, going to the door. "I'm not expecting anyone. It's probably someone selling something."

Marlene followed Rachel to the door. "Not on Christmas Eve, hon. You get the door and I'll just slip right on out like a quiet little mouse."

"That's ridiculous, Marlene. You stay." Rachel opened the door and stared up at David, standing on the porch with an armload of gifts. She felt her heart lift with happiness at the sight of him, then quickly looked away, afraid he would see too much of her feelings revealed in her expression. For a moment she couldn't think of a thing to say.

Marlene said it for her. "David, what a wonderful surprise! You come right in. I'm just leaving. On my way out the door right now. You go on in and make yourself at home."

David stepped inside, giving Marlene a slight nod as she passed by. "Thanks, Marlene. Merry Christmas."

Marlene was already halfway to her condo when she called back meaningfully, "I sure hope it'll be a merry Christmas for you, too, David."

"What'd Marlene mean by that?" David kicked the door shut behind him and released his armload of bright, foil-wrapped packages on the coffee table. "Marlene sounds in her usual good spirits," he remarked irritably.

"You know Marlene. Always a trouper. Nothing gets her down."

"Cute little tree," he said, nodding at her bedraggled artificial pine.

"Yeah, I decided a real tree was too much work this year." Why was she bothering to explain herself? Why didn't she just say *What woman wants to bother decorating a tree when her husband's out running around on her?*

An awkward silence settled between them. Rachel hugged herself, her arms resting on the obvious swell of her belly. She was wearing a silk caftan David had always liked, but now it felt too intimate, too revealing. It was a silly feeling. Everything was covered. Why did she feel so exposed? She gazed down at the gifts. "Well, it looks like Santa's come early," she murmured, trying to sound nonchalant, all the while wondering if Kit had picked out the gifts. "You really shouldn't have, David."

"Why not? You and Brian are still my family. Did you think I'd let Christmas go by without bringing you gifts?"

"I didn't know what to think," she admitted.

"I may be a jerk, but not that big a jerk." He sat down in his recliner, not settling back but remaining on the edge of the chair, his hands on his knees, as if he might jump up at any moment and escape. "I even threw in a couple of things for the baby. Of course, not knowing whether it's a boy or girl, I was limited in my choices. So everything's yellow. You can take it all back after the baby comes if you want to." He smiled, but it was forced. He obviously felt as uncomfortable as she did.

"Would you like some coffee? Or a Coke?"

"No, thanks. I'm fine."

"Have you eaten?"

"Yeah, I'm all set. Don't worry about me."

He probably had had a romantic candlelight dinner with Kit in some fancy restaurant, she mused darkly. She sat down on the sofa across from him and self-consciously smoothed the silky folds of her caftan. She wished she'd taken more time with her makeup and hair. She had hastily applied some foundation and blusher and run a brush through her thick curls, but she was far from making a dazzling fashion statement. The last thing she wanted to look like was a sloppy, pregnant housewife. "If you came to see Brian, he's in his room. Probably already in some Internet chat room talking with someone from Outer Mongolia."

David smiled. "It figures. I think our boy's obsessed by that computer."

"I know. I try to keep tabs on him, but I don't want him to think I'm trying to invade his privacy." She stood uncertainly. "Listen, I'll go get him. I'm sure he's the one you came to see. He'll be glad to see you, too."

"No, that's okay," said David quickly. "Listen, Rae, I came to see you, too. Sit down a minute. We haven't talked for a while. I'd like to know how you're doing."

"Doing?" She stared blankly at him. What did he expect her to say? I'm facing single motherhood because you're letting another woman break up our marriage, but other than that I'm terrific?

"I mean, are you feeling okay? Is everything going all right with your pregnancy?"

"Yes, David, I'm fine. The baby's fine."

"Good," he said with a sigh of relief. "I worry

about you, you know. I keep remembering the rough time you had when Brian was born."

So he remembers, she thought.

"You look great, Rae. You have that healthy glow people talk about."

"I do?" Her cheeks grew warm. Was she still attractive to David after all?

"You looked the same way when you were expecting Brian. Remember? I used to tease you about it. I said, if we could bottle that kind of beauty, we'd make a million dollars."

"Yes, I do remember," she said softly. "You even said it when I was nine months pregnant and big as a house. I figured you were just trying to make me feel better."

"No, I was dead serious. You always had that inner glow about you. It was better than anything Hollywood could come up with." Slowly, tentatively, David moved from his recliner over to the sofa. He turned to face her and took her hand in his, his very presence making her weak, turning her heart to gelatin. "Rachel, sweetheart, I've been so worried about you. It's Christmas and I hate this animosity between us. Isn't there something we can do to resolve this? You know the old saying, 'Peace on earth, good will to men.'"

Tears gathered behind Rachel's eyes. She yearned to collapse into David's arms and pretend these bitter weeks apart had never happened, that this was like every other Christmas they had spent together, like all the Christmases they would spend together for the rest of their lives. "Oh, David," she said, sighing. No other words would come.

He moved toward her and gathered her into his

arms. His warm, solid closeness dazzled her—the familiar, intoxicating smell of his skin, his tangy lime aftershave, his sweet breath on her cheek. She wanted nothing more than for him to sweep her up in his arms and carry her to their room for a night of tender passion.

But even as he sought her mouth, the voice of reason struggled to the surface of her emotions and she heard herself say, "No, David, we can't. Too much has happened. Nothing's resolved."

He released her and sat back, emitting a heavy sigh. "I'm sorry, Rachel. That wasn't fair, I know." He pulled a linen handkerchief from his shirt pocket and blotted his upper lip. "I guess it's the holidays. Christmas and all that. The time of year when you believe anything's possible. I guess for a moment I forgot reality and got caught up in the enchantment."

Rachel studied his ruggedly handsome profile. She loved every line and angle of that face, but there were aspects to it now that were unfamiliar to her. She didn't know this man anymore. He was a stranger to her. "Making love won't solve the problems between us, David," she said in a small, wounded voice.

He stood and straightened his jacket, his expression stony, inscrutable. His voice took on an edge of bitter sarcasm. "You're right as usual, Rae. It'll take more than love to make things right between us. And whatever it takes, I obviously don't have it."

Chapter Eleven

Her thoughts are running wild, straying off to nowhere. There is a hall, certainly a hall, very long, very mysterious. It is like a throat, with the narrow inner warmth of a throat. She is dazed by the warmth, her eyes pressed up against the darkness. She runs against the darkness, a frenzied running, with her thoughts trailing like kite string. She keeps running. What is this madness? She hears voices, pinpoints of sound, faint and distant, distressing somehow. The voices of men. What are they saying? She can do nothing about the voices; they terrify her. She is screaming, ''David, Brian, David!''

Rachel woke with a start. She sat up, trembling, then lay back down, sighing relief. A dream, a stupid, hideous dream, she thought. I have been dreaming, that's all—just dreaming!

Rachel rolled over and stared at the clock on the nightstand. Nearly eight in the morning. The first Saturday of February. She listened. The house was full of a silence that she recognized and accepted now—

the lack of a man in the house, a man's sounds, his special noises that one takes for granted when they are there and misses when they are gone.

There was another silence, too, which Rachel understood as Brian's absence. No doubt Brian had risen and dressed and left the house soundlessly, so that he would not disturb his mother. He had gone to Ronnie's, or the two of them had gone off somewhere together doing who knew what as the day was just beginning. Brian rarely ran with the church crowd anymore. Rachel wondered if he was somehow trying to punish his parents for their breakup. Brian would be gone until lunchtime, when he would suddenly appear, eat the meal Rachel provided, then wait patiently, wordlessly, for his father to arrive for their regular weekend excursion. This had become the pattern of things, the Saturday pattern.

It was a dream, she thought again—the hall, the voices, the running. It was nothing, a dream. What did it mean? Nothing, nothing!

Rachel had no desire to get out of bed. Her body was heavy, sluggish; it kept her down, prevented her from walking light and free. She had been putting on too much weight lately—three pounds over the Christmas holidays, nearly two pounds a week during the month of January. This would have to stop; she must do better during February. How could she be putting on so much weight? The baby was less than six months along. How big would she be by nine months?

For an instant she recalled the woman in the doctor's office during her first visit. That woman, who had been due at any moment, had been no part of Rachel then, just an object of curiosity. Now Rachel felt as if she were that woman, or soon would be. Rachel could not escape this baby, could not stop the processes inside her that continued relentlessly day and night creating a baby for her. She was part of the process, had become the process. Her own identity was slipping away, losing itself to the baby, whatever the baby was.

The baby was no longer an idea in her mind, no longer a mere theory lacking physical substance. She could feel this baby—he had a lot to do and he did not want her to rest. It seemed that his legs and arms moved constantly; he was anxious to get going, to get things done. Even now, as Rachel lay on her back very still on the bed, she watched with fascination the gentle rolling movements on the surface of her abdomen. The baby shifted and turned and made small hills and silly angles of her stomach. It awed her to think of this tiny baby inhabiting the most secret center of her body. How could such a thing be?

Rachel made herself get out of bed. The morning offered her nothing, but she had to face it. She had to do something with it, get it behind her, over and done with.

She thought again that she should contact the lawyer. She was always putting it off. She should go ahead and get the divorce. At least start things rolling. Make the first move. She considered this while she poured herself some coffee. She should get the divorce from David and make the final break. Perhaps she would feel better. Perhaps her life would not seem so suspended, so flimsy. Perhaps life would take on some direction again. It was possible.

Of course, she was still dependent on David for financial support, but after the baby came, she could go back to school and get the counseling degree she had always dreamed of. With her M.F.C.C. degree, she could seriously pursue a career in drama therapy. Women were forging careers for themselves all the time. Surely she could take care of herself—and of Brian and the baby. They would manage just fine without David.

Rachel sipped her coffee and reasoned that, on the other hand, perhaps it was just as well to let David take the first step. If he decided he wanted this girl, this Kit Kincaid, let him get the divorce. Why should she do it for him?

Rachel frowned into her coffee. She hated herself when she was like this. Her bitterness was like a dark thread sewing up her emotions. All of her feelings were tainted by it. There was nothing she could do. She was trapped, and her senses grew murky trying to reason it out.

In her head, Rachel knew that she was a Christian. The Holy Spirit lived inside her, no one had to tell her this. But she also knew that God's Spirit was having a hard time saying anything to her now. She didn't seem able to listen. Where was He, this Holy Spirit of God, that He couldn't be heard? That His voice was so small, like an echo? Had she, Rachel, done this to Him? Was she stifling this Spirit inside her? What could she do about it? She was on a particular course, a certain inevitable track, and how could she change anything now?

Rachel had prayed for her husband for years. She had trusted God that David would someday accept her faith as his own. Now David was all but out of her life; he was like a candle going out and almost gone. What could she possibly do about him now?

And Brian. She had taken Brian to church since he was eight, almost half of his life. She had resolved that he would not be like his father, a man without faith in Christ. She had done everything she could do. Now Brian was slipping away, shutting her out, becoming a stranger to her. In January he had given up his Sunday school office and his duties as social chairman of his youth group. He skipped church whenever possible, whenever Rachel would let him get away with it. When she forced him to go, he trudged silently behind her, like a sulking prisoner, a man condemned. How could this be? What terrible thing was wrong with Brian?

Rachel rinsed out her coffee cup, went into the living room and sat down in David's recliner. She was always tired now, needing to sit down frequently, needing to rest. She was constantly aware of her body—its demands, its pervading weaknesses, the overwhelming limitations of her body. Would she ever be free again? Would her spirit be free?

Rachel felt a stab of regret, a feeling she could not define or touch with her thinking. It had something to do with her love for Christ and her inability to claim His power, the power He certainly wanted her to have. Why did she always fall so far short of what He wanted?

Rachel had not prayed for a very long time. She had occasionally mouthed prayers—glib phrases that fell into place without thought, small talk in the presence of God. She recognized the futility of such prayer, for the tone of her voice was much like the inevitable tone of the conversations she had with David. Nothing real was ever said; nothing real was alluded to. Words skimmed the surface, rarely touching a significant base. It was that way now with God; she rarely touched base with Him, rarely made connections. Her words fell flat. Where was God that she could no longer reach Him?

She could attempt to pray. She could try to break through the wall she had built around herself, the willfulness and resentment of her own heart. She could do that.

But I don't know what to say, she thought, aware of a vague stirring of panic. What if she couldn't get through, could never again get through to God? Was she doomed to face all the mornings of her life like this one—without meaning or purpose or joy? Gray, tasteless mornings? Was that her fate?

"Dear God," she said aloud, her voice filling up the silent spaces of the house. "Dear God, I don't know what to say to You anymore. I love You, but I don't know how to reach You. Help me, please help me."

There was a fragile responsiveness rising in her heart, a familiar sense of surrender beginning to wash over her. Good. It was working. Her prayers were working. Now, if only God would cleanse the deep, private recesses of her soul. Could it be that simple? Could she be clean again? Dear God, she longed to be clean.

Her words faltered. Her throat was closing up. She had nothing to give to God. How could she pray? She tried to think of something worthwhile to say, but nothing came to mind. What was she thinking of, thinking she could ever please God? Why not give up, forget it, leave God alone?

Warm tears stuck to her lashes, spilling out. She brushed at them with her hand. Now she would have to blow her nose. Was there a tissue in her bathrobe pocket?

"Dear God, I'm sorry," she said, fumbling with the tissue, blowing her nose. "I need You so much, but I can't change anything, not even myself. I've been so filled with anger and bitterness against David, I can't even reach You anymore. Please don't be a stranger to me. Please take charge. I give You all that I am, the whole mess of my life, even my anger and pride. And I give you David and Brian, too. They are strangers to me—we are all strangers. It breaks my heart, Lord. I don't know what to do or where to turn. I just know I can't handle it anymore. Please, God, do what You want with me. I'm Your needy child."

Chapter Twelve

It was early February, a warm evening even by Southern California's standards. Marlene Benson opened a can of chunky vegetable soup and emptied the contents into a saucepan on the stove. She added a little water, although this was not required. She turned on the gas so that a bright blue flame erupted under the saucepan, then stirred the water gently into the soup. She took a slice of bread from the freezer and set it on a plate to thaw. She always kept a loaf in the freezer to keep it fresh, since she used only a slice or two at a time. A loaf of bread could last her two weeks or more.

While the soup simmered and the bread thawed, Marlene set up a TV tray in front of the sofa in the living room. It was a metal tray imprinted with a Matisse-style painting of orange and yellow flowers, daisies or something, but in places the flowers were worn away and dull metal showed through. At times it seemed to Marlene that everything she owned was wearing away, growing dull. She checked the TV guide to see what was on. One of those new law-and-order shows was playing, plus a medical drama and a couple of sitcoms, and a Ginger Rogers movie made in 1942. She chose the movie.

Marlene went back to her kitchen and spread diet margarine on the thawed bread. She was putting on more weight again. She could feel a thickening around her waist and hips. So she would try a new diet, although she supposed it would last no longer than most of her self-imposed diets. She considered a moment and then yielded to the temptation to spread a generous layer of grape jelly on the bread before carrying her meager supper to the living room.

Start the diet tomorrow, she thought. She could be quite philosophical about it, for there was really no one who cared whether she lost or gained ten or twenty pounds. It was highly unlikely anyone would look her up and down and exclaim, "Oh, Marlene, dear, you're putting on weight." If she lost a few pounds, someone might venture to say, "Why, Marlene, you look thinner, how marvelous!" But more likely no one would say anything one way or the other, whether she looked like a blimp or like Twiggy. So the jelly really didn't matter.

There was a pattern to Marlene's days, a strict routine that rarely varied, the sort of schedule people living alone set for themselves. She probably would have denied it with an alarmed wave of the hand, for she liked to think of herself as free to choose how her life would be and what she would do each day. Nevertheless, she rarely changed the sequence of her activities or the time delegated to each endeavor.

Marlene was free in one sense, for she had no one to please but herself, no one to make concessions to, since that dreadful day eight years ago when her husband had died. She remembered that day as if it were yesterday. One moment she and Harry had been talking. He was telling her a joke, halfway through, and laughing already at the punch line. Suddenly he stopped laughing and clutched his chest. She thought it was part of the joke and began to laugh, until Harry collapsed beside her, blank eyed, unmoving.

Later she thought about the irony of it all—that her darling Harry, who loved humor almost as much as he loved to eat, had died telling a joke. To this day she didn't know the punch line, although at times she tried to imagine what Harry was going to say, how he had planned to finish the story. Some folks told her she should be glad Harry had died doing what he loved—laughing and telling one of his tall tales. Gradually Marlene realized the truth of their remark, but for a long time she was angry at God for playing such a permanent practical joke on her Harry. Now, however, she figured the first thing she was going to ask Harry in Glory was, "Okay, already, Harry, you've had long enough. What's the punch line?"

So until the day she joined Harry and met her Maker, Marlene had no one but herself to answer to and depend on.

Then again, she reflected with some amusement and discomposure, there was someone—or could be someone—special in her life. But at the moment he hardly counted. In fact, he probably didn't even know Marlene's last name, to show how much he counted! But if truth be told, she cared for him more than she wished to admit. Mr. Timmons, Stanley Timmons, an usher at church, was a shy, pleasant-faced, middle-aged bachelor with thin wisps of graying hair and round, black, plastic-rimmed glasses sliding halfway down his nose. Marlene often felt an impulse to push his glasses up for him to the top of his nose, but since their conversation was usually limited to a formal "Good morning" or "Good evening, how are you tonight?" she would surely never attempt such a thing.

Periodically Marlene prayed that Mr. Timmons might notice her and realize what fine qualities she possessed—that it might suddenly dawn on him that here was the kind of Christian woman he needed. Still, Mr. Timmons offered her only a rather stiff "Good morning" each Sunday before passing out of her life for another week. Each week she put her all into that "Good morning, Mr. Timmons, how are you today?" But all for naught. It was rather hopeless, she thought dismally, taking mouthfuls of soup.

This night was like any other night, like *every* other night for Marlene—eating her dinner while watching TV, nothing expected of her, no one demanding anything in particular, the whole world leaving her to the quietness of familiar walls and overstuffed furniture. Her life was like an old song played over and over—the same quiet dinners and TV and her own private thoughts, going over the day and wondering about all the days ahead. The same thoughts played over and over, different and still the same.

Marlene Benson had a particular closeness to God that prevented her from feeling her life was meaningless. If anything, she considered herself in a state of waiting, of suspension perhaps. At any moment, at the signal of the Lord Himself, the waiting would be over, things would click into place and the wheels of her life would begin to revolve. She was certain of this and waited for it patiently.

In the meantime, she kept busy, and she accomplished a great many things. She worked as an executive secretary for a computer firm in downtown Long Beach. She was Sunday school teacher for eighth-grade girls and was on several of the committees for the Women's Fellowship and the Missionary Guild. She had a full life—people would certainly agree she had enough to keep her busy.

Marlene enjoyed being busy and she enjoyed people. She knew folks considered her a bit bold and aggressive, even a little mouthy at times. So okay, she was an extrovert at heart, never at a loss for words, ready for anything, a good sport. Good old Marlene. She could be counted on, Marlene could. She always did her part, did what she felt were her duties before God. But as the years passed since her husband's death, she became increasingly aware that she was more comfortable with God than with people.

Around other people it was necessary to be many things—neat, attractive, properly attired, polite, saying and doing whatever was appropriate for the persons and circumstances involved. But Marlene had never found it easy to be attractive. Comical, the life of the party, someone's big sister, all of these, yes. But attractive...no. She had never felt pretty. And though she ritualistically followed the rules of good grooming, she never escaped a certain sense of awkwardness, a feeling that something about her body was not quite right. She ignored the feeling, lived with it, laughed at it. Laughed at herself. Even made jokes about her weight to put others at ease: "Hey,

I'm a size eight personality trapped in a size sixteen body. Get me out!"

Only when she was alone with God did Marlene feel lusciously content. Accepted. Loved. When she prayed, she was beautiful; she knew it. She felt beautiful before God, and the thought of it warmed her. She knew this was merely a glimpse of how it would be in heaven when she had her transformed body, and this, too, was something she must wait for. In the meantime, she loved the Lord with a fierce devotion and waited for the things she knew would someday come to her—a gorgeous body, the rest of Harry's joke, a glimpse of her Savior and Lord.

This particular night was foggy, quiet except for the occasional muted blasts of a foghorn from the harbor. It was less than a week before St. Valentine's Day. On Valentine's Day, at seven in the evening, there would be a sweetheart banquet in the Christian education building adjoining the church—ten dollars per person, with an appetizing menu including Swiss steak, fresh peas and real mashed potatoes with gravy. The guest speaker was a missionary on furlough from the Philippines. Perhaps Mr. Timmons would attend the banquet. Perhaps he would sit near her. Perhaps they would talk. Perhaps…or he might not come at all. She would not think of that.

It was Marlene's responsibility to prepare name cards for the sweetheart banquet. She could have made them on her computer, but she decided to try something more creative. She had colored paper and scissors and black marking pens ready. She had a list of names of people who had signed up to attend. Mr. Timmons's name was not on the list, but that meant nothing. Only that he had not given the church secretary his name, that he had not yet purchased his ticket. He had time—almost a week. She had time; she was good at waiting.

Marlene was sorting the sheets of colored paper when she heard the first sound—a car pulling up outside, the engine turned off. She ignored it, busy with her paper. She was expecting no one; the sound was forgotten. Then, a little while later, Marlene heard the slamming of a car door. This was nothing, either. Car doors slammed all the time. But then something else: footsteps on the sidewalk, a shuffling of feet, a sound at her door, a sudden insistent knocking. Marlene jumped up, startled, and dropped the colored paper on the desk.

"Who—?" she said. She moved toward the door, listening. The knock stopped for a moment, then began again, harder.

Marlene felt an unreasonable fear shoot through her chest. No one ever came to see her with such a hard knock on her door. People who came to see her knocked gently, a careful, pleasant knock with pauses between, so that she could answer. No one ever wanted her enough to knock so heavily, with such apparent intensity. What was going on?

Marlene slipped the chain lock into place on the door and peered through a narrow slit in the curtains. A man stood outside. It was too dark to determine his identity, but something in his stance suggested David Webber. Marlene peeked again. Yes. Yes, David Webber. What did he want? She opened the door a crack. The chain lock was in place. She said softly, "David? David Webber? Is that you out there?"

Was he startled by her voice? He moved backward suddenly, stepping awkwardly, almost losing his footing. "What? David Webber, all right," he said loudly. "Where were you? I kept knocking—"

"I'm sorry, David. What do you want?"

"Want? I want to talk to you, Marlene. You and I have to talk."

Marlene knew David was angry, but she wasn't afraid to let him in. Maybe it was time that they had an honest talk together. Still, she hesitated to open the door all the way. "Have you seen Rachel?" she asked, stalling, trying to decide exactly how to handle him.

"Rachel?" he mumbled. "No, why should I see Rachel? I drove over here to my condo, but I don't live here anymore. Don't you know that?"

There was a terrible hollowness to David's voice, a gloom, something faintly desperate behind his words—perhaps a cry for help, thought Marlene. She removed the chain and opened the door. "Come in," she said.

"That's better," said David, stepping inside. He was wearing a white dress shirt and slacks. Marlene drew back, startled by his face, by the lines of haggardness and shadows around his eyes. He wore a sullen, downcast expression around the mouth. He looked weary. Defeated.

He crossed the room and sat down heavily on the sofa. "This is good," he said, sighing deeply. "I had to sit down. My legs feel like rubber. My head's a balloon. I'm a mess, a real stinking mess."

"I'll get you some coffee, David. Just sit there—"

"No. No coffee. I want to talk to you. Sit down, Marlene. Be a good girl and just sit down."

She sat down, then leaned forward a little, her hands folded in her lap. There was a primness about the way she sat, a deliberate formality, as if this would protect her. She sat quietly, waiting. In a moment she could jump up. She could run. She could scream. "What do we have to talk about?" she asked, her voice amazingly calm.

"I have news," he said, his voice heavy with sarcasm. "My company regretted to inform me I am no longer working. They call it downsizing. Too many cutbacks. What they mean is, no more job. That's it—kaput! My services are no longer needed, simple as that. I didn't clean out my desk or anything. I just went out and drove around. I've been driving for hours, and ended up here, of all places," he added with a harsh laugh.

"You were laid off?"

"Laid off? Yeah, laid off. Canned. Like Russian roulette. I knew my turn was coming. Just a matter of time, that's all. That's all anything is—a matter of time."

"You're sure you don't want some coffee?"

"No coffee! I said no coffee, didn't I? A man loses everything he has—his family, his home, his job—and people want to give him coffee. What is this coffee? How is coffee going to help me?"

He was right. She had to drop the platitudes and be more honest with him.

"David, does Rachel know about your job?"

He shook his head dazedly. "No. What's it to her? Money? I'll get money for her. I'll find something, some job."

"I'm sorry, David. I don't know what to say...."

He waved his hand in the air. "Say nothing. What's it to you? You and Rachel—what do either of you have to do with me? I don't know why I came here."

"I wish I could help."

He sat forward staring at her with a frightening intensity. "Oh, you helped all right, lady. You helped a long time ago when you filled Rachel's head with all that garbage. Religion, church, believe this, believe that. She was fine until you came along—fine, I tell you."

Then his angry stare changed. He looked imploringly at her, the way a dying man might look, like a man full of unspeakable torment. "What did you do to her, Marlene?" he asked, anguished, the words catching somewhere in his throat. "She never came back, never came back to me after she got mixed up with you. What did you do?"

"I didn't do anything, David," Marlene answered softly, groping for words. "I just showed her how to accept Christ as her Savior, that's all I did."

"She never came back, not really. She was never the same."

"That had nothing to do with me, David. God changed her. She gave herself to God. That made the difference."

"That made her shut me out? What kind of God is that, breaking up families, wrecking homes? Answer me that, will you?"

"But David, Rachel wanted you to share her faith. She wanted that more than anything in the world."

David sank back against the sofa cushions and closed his eyes. "She took Brian, and the two of them went their own way. Sometimes I almost hated her. It bugged me, not being the most important thing in her life anymore. I couldn't compete with this God of hers. How could I compete? I was a poor second, that's what I was. There was always this barrier between us."

Marlene sat forward, her tone earnest, urgent. "It didn't have to be that way, David. It doesn't have to be now. Christ loves you as much as He loves Rachel."

David waved her off. "No, don't start on me, Marlene. I don't want to hear it. This God of yours, this loving God, took everything away from me—my home, my wife, my son and now my job. What kind of God is that? I think your God would like to finish me off, that's what I think."

"You feel that way because you're beating your head against Him, and against His love," said Marlene, holding her own emotion in check. "He's trying to reach you, David. These trials are God's way of getting your attention, making you realize your need—"

"My need is to get out of here," David declared hoarsely. He hoisted himself to his feet and headed for the door. "You're crazy, you're a crazy woman," he said, fumbling with the doorknob.

"David, please, listen to me. Why don't you talk to Pastor Emrick? Maybe he can help you understand."

He stared at her for a long moment with haunted eyes filled with despair and loathing. Then he stormed out the door, slamming it behind him. "Crazy, crazy woman!" Marlene heard him exclaim to the night.

Chapter Thirteen

It was the first week of March, a cool evening. The air was very still. David Webber unlocked the door to his apartment and went in, flicking the light switch as he entered. The overhead bulb jarred away the darkness and bathed the room with a smooth sallow light that brought things into focus. The room smelled stale, closed up; it was a dark box that shunned air.

David removed his sports coat and slipped it over a hanger in the closet, straightening the collar and the sleeves. Somehow the material felt worn and sleazy, although it was an expensive jacket.

This place was an eyesore, a cheap, one-bedroom, furnished apartment, something he could afford. The furniture was light and colorless, having no personality, mere sticks of polished wood arranged and fastened with glue in angles resembling furniture—a chair, a sofa, end tables. David had as little to do with this place as he could; he did not allow himself to become a part of it. When he sat down, he remained on the surface, not relaxing, not letting himself find comfort in this furniture that was not his own. This was not home, nothing like his home.

Somewhere else, only miles away, was his home, a place that was still part of him, though he did not belong there now. In that other place were his wife and son, going about their business, doing the things people do every day—without him. Four months ago he—David Webber—had been relegated to this apartment. He had spent hours in this new place, hating it, fearful that somehow it might become a permanent thing, a place he would never escape.

Thinking about it now, he could almost be amused; he could almost smile at the dread he had had of these rooms. Now, tonight, this fine March night, even the dreariness of the walls did not bother him. He was immune. He could walk through the rooms of the place and not be touched. He would not suffocate. He was breathing, and he would not have to worry about his breath again.

He was free and did not even know yet what it meant—free!

Bound by the limitations of his body and his mind and this apartment, feeling keenly the loss of Rachel and his son and his job, his dignity and his selfhood threatened and his future hanging by a thread—still, he was free. What did that mean? What really did it mean? Free.

David went to the kitchen for a glass of milk. He took the milk and a box of crackers with him to the living room and sat down. The crackers were slightly stale and made no sound when he ate them. This place that he hated was silent for a change, silent in all of its parts, waiting for him to sort and arrange all his thoughts. This apartment would not threaten him again, he knew that. That part of his life was over—the threat of things that might devour him, of things that had no end.

He thought back, going over the day's chain of events, the innocuous activities leading up without warning to this new thing, this sudden freedom he could not comprehend. He remembered that the day had started badly. He'd had nothing to do, no reason for getting out of bed. It was getting to him, this having no job. It was getting him down. He was displaced and floating, with no strings to tie him to anything. He needed ties, but there was nothing, only the irrelevant continuity of days and nights—days without meaning, nights without rest. And the needs, endless and vaguely disturbing—the need to eat, to shave, to dress and undress, and the need to come to something at last, to make some sense of being a man, of living.

He wondered what had brought him to this place where he was now, to this empty endless moment with its terrible demands. What had brought him here and what could he do about it? Or was he helpless, destined forever to be a thirty-five-year-old man with no home, no family and no peace?

Those had been his thoughts this morning. He had shaved and dressed, his mind sullen, his body sluggish, like an old man who had nowhere to go. Why should he be like an old man to whom everything in life had already happened? He fixed breakfast for himself—bacon and eggs and coffee—although he was not hungry and had no desire for the taste of food.

He left his apartment before noon and went to the corner for a newspaper. It was a ritual. He scanned the classified ads, his eyes moving hungrily down each column. There was nothing for him; he did not really expect anything. Rumor was that hundreds of engineers were applying for a single civil service job, or any job—a gardener, clerk, gas station attendant. David suspected the rumors were true. With all the recent aerospace megamergers, takeovers and layoffs, no one wanted engineers.

When he had finished with the morning paper each day, he went for a walk, as if he actually had somewhere to go. Some days he drove around to various companies in the area, going in the door with a confident stride, asking the receptionist if he could see the personnel manager. Or could he fill out an application or leave his résumé?

The women who greeted him were always polite. They listened, watching him with clear, alert eyes. They took his résumé and let him take an application blank to fill out. But their smiles said there was nothing. They could afford such charity, for they knew what he knew: he was wasting his time. Nevertheless, he appreciated their smiles and returned them generously, maintaining for these women a facade of optimism.

This morning, however, he didn't play that game. He would not go through the motions. Instead, he walked and let his thoughts carry him where they would. He thought a great deal about his life and about his wife and son and the baby to come. It bothered him that not only had his own life been upset by the events of the past few months, but his wife and son had been wounded deeply, as well.

It seemed he hardly knew Rachel now since their separation. She avoided him, demonstrating a coldness he knew sprang from the hurt she felt. And the knowledge that she had been desperate enough at one point to consider an abortion was more painful than David cared to admit. But that was in the past now. Rachel would be all right. She would manage.

But what about Brian? He had changed during the past few weeks, in ways David could not explain. On the surface they got along, talked, had a good time together. But on another level, Brian was different, older, growing increasingly remote.

Besides, there had been incidents that had raised nagging questions in David's mind. For instance, the day he'd picked Brian up at school to take him to Long Beach Harbor to visit the Queen Mary. Brian had become sick and had to go home. Was it really just something he had eaten? Or could it have been something else? Did David only imagine the signs?

Then there was the evening he and Brian were having a purely academic discussion about the legalization of marijuana. They were drinking milk shakes and munching fries when a news blurb on the subject come over the radio. In minutes, Brian's face became animated and his voice rose heatedly. Why should the possession of marijuana be an illegal act? How was pot really any worse than cigarettes or liquor? Why couldn't people decide for themselves what they wanted to do?

David, hiding his surprise and concern, remarked only that he hoped Brian would never get involved in drugs. When Brian made no attempt to reply, David persisted. He hoped Brian would have the good sense to leave drugs alone. What had tormented David since that evening was that Brian never gave him an answer, never said a word. David was left with his own nagging, growing suspicions. Did Brian need help? What could David do?

As David continued to walk, his thoughts turned to the baby, a child destined to be a stranger to him. What could he do for this child when he could not even help himself? Soberly, thoughtfully, David considered the entire pattern of his life, going step by step over all the events that had brought him to this present moment.

He reflected that he had done a great deal with his life and yet now he had nothing. It was as if he had to start all over, building a new identity, a new man to take the place of David Webber. But how could he do this? He was who he was, the result of thirty-five years of experiences, the product of his own actions and attitudes.

He realized dismally that he could not unwrap a single hour of his life and rewrap it into a different mold with a new, more pleasing shape. He could change nothing of the past; he was locked into the present moment. And already the future was slipping over him, confusing him, a filmy web of weird mosaics. By the time he was freed from the tangle of it all, it would be gone, dissolved, just more of the past to puzzle over and finally forget. Things were inevitable, the whole course of life. There was only so much anyone could do. It was never enough.

David had walked this afternoon until his feet hurt. At last he had given up and gone back to his apartment to sit by the window looking out, waiting for something, anything to happen. He thought about the day he was laid off—was it really less than a month ago, not years?—the shock of it, that he could actually be one of the guys laid off. The astonishment persisted, even now, buried somewhere. Why had it been such a shock?

He thought about the fact that Kit had not been laid off. She was still needed. They had work for her to do, and—it was funny—work was not really important to Kit. She was conscientious, going each day to the office and doing her work well, but she would just as soon not have worked at all, if she didn't have to. Funny, yes.

David had not seen much of Kit lately. What was there to say to her? What was the use of seeing her? After he and Rachel separated, he had dated Kit occasionally, but their relationship didn't seem to be going anywhere. It baffled him. He had been on the verge of falling in love with her and had admitted as much to Rachel.

But then, something happened; nothing happened. What was it? Was it that he could not commit himself? Was he unwilling to push his life impulsively into some new mold when all of the separate parts of his life were so unsettled? He could love Kit, but did he want that love to take charge of him, possess him? Or, bottom line, was the love he thought he felt for Kit just physical attraction or an ego trip? Was he drawn to her because she knew exactly how to feed his vanity? He hadn't let himself believe he could be so shallow and self-absorbed, but that possibility hung heavily on him now.

Kit had apparently sensed David's doubts and confusion; she had left him to himself and, during office hours, had remained friendly and completely unruffled. But now that he no longer saw her at the office, there seemed even less reason to see her socially. Perhaps someday when things were straightened out in his personal life, he could sort out his feelings for Kit Kincaid.

David spent the afternoon thinking about being laid off, recalling how he'd stalked out of the office that terrible day and headed for his car. He had driven around for hours, then had headed for the condominium where Rachel and Brian lived. He'd sat in the car in front of the condo nearly half an hour, dazed, his thoughts muddled. He'd realized he could not go to Rachel, but he had driven to this place. Why? What was here for him?

At last he had gotten out of the car and gone to the door of the neighboring condo, where Marlene Benson lived. He had knocked loudly on the door, needing to be heard. Haltingly, with trepidation, Marlene had taken him in, had listened to him and talked to him. What had she said? It was fuzzy. Nothing she had said remained with him, except one thing—she had begged him to go see her pastor. Talk to him, she'd said.

The idea had remained lodged somewhere in David's head. And so this afternoon, while he had sat by the window looking out, waiting for something to happen—on this fine March day the memory of her words had come to him, and he'd thought, *That is something I can do!*

Now it was evening. He was in his apartment, sitting on his sofa eating stale crackers and drinking milk, marveling over the fact that he was finally free. He was still in a state of astonishment, dazed at what he had done. How had it come about, this new freedom? How did it happen?

He considered the evening, savoring the memory of the past few hours. Earlier in the evening he had gone to see Pastor Emrick, Marlene and Rachel's pastor, and had sat with him in his study for several hours, telling this man he hardly knew the whole story of his life. And when it had come time for Pastor Emrick to speak, something happened inside David. For the very first time, he understood. It wasn't his imagination. He was responding to the verses the minister read from the Bible. At first he was mildly surprised at himself, at the receptiveness he felt inside. What was going on, that suddenly he had an appetite for this sort of thing—for religion, for God?

Then the response expanded. As Pastor Emrick explained what Jesus Christ had done for him, David was aware of a hunger sweeping over him, stretching through his mind, absorbing his entire imagination. He was convinced now that he had a soul, for this

Get 2

*W*e'd like to send you two free books to introduce you to ***Love Inspired***. **Your two books have a combined cover price of $9.00, but they are yours free! We'll even send you a wonderful thank-you gift—the elegant jewelry box shown below.**

Both of your free *Love Inspired* novels are filled with joy, faith and true Christian values. Th stories will lift your spirits and gladden your heart! There's no cost. No risk. No obligation t buy anything, ever.

SPECIAL FREE GIFT!

Steeple Hill®

We'll send you this elegant heart-shaped jewelry box, absolutely FREE, just for giving *Love Inspired* a try! Don't miss out—mail the reply card today!

idea of Christ rescuing him had electrified an unknown part of him. The sensation pleased and intrigued him.

He accepted the pastor's suggestion that they kneel and pray together, that David confess his sins and ask Christ into his heart and claim Christ's gift of eternal life. It was done in a moment and David got off his knees without a word and with little emotion in him.

There was instead within his mind a lucidness, a clarity of perception, a certain recognition of something vital. He had finally found an answer, *the* Answer. All his life the meaning of living had escaped him. Life was a puzzle. One could assemble many pieces of it in a lifetime, coming up with various meanings as the pieces fit together.

But a person could not see the entire picture or learn the essential meaning of life until he or she grasped the crucial piece that made the puzzle complete. Why had he never seen it before? Christ was the missing piece, the all-important key. Without Him life was incomplete; the meaning of living could not be comprehended. Now, for the first time, David had the whole picture. He had all the pieces, and all the pieces fit!

Into David's mind flashed a clear image of something from a book he had read in school as a youngster—John Bunyan's *Pilgrim's Progress.* He recalled that Christian carried a heavy burden on his back, his load of sins, but as soon as he reached the cross, the burden tumbled from his shoulders and Christian was light and free and joyful. The story had always amused David a little, for certainly, life was not like that; he hadn't even sensed he carried any burden back then.

Now, however, he had to admit to a certain sensation of lightness and liberty. He was a new man in Christ. He rejoiced in his heart. It was a fact. He was free.

David Webber returned the box of stale crackers and the empty milk glass to the kitchen, marveling as he went at his new freedom, his redemption. Imagine it, imagine being free.

Chapter Fourteen

David glanced at his watch. Not quite seven. Might have known he'd be early. Too bad—Kit was not known for her promptness. He would probably have to wait for her, sitting around while she fussed with her makeup or something. He wanted to get on with this evening. There were things he had to say to Kit, things she would have to know. He didn't want to waste time on trifles, not tonight.

Rapping on her apartment door, he thought ruefully that it would be just his luck for Kit's roommate to be home. She was a pain, that girl. She never shut up. He hoped she was off somewhere for the evening. David needed peace tonight so he could keep his thoughts in order. He had certain things he needed to say.

The door opened. Sure enough, it was Kit's roommate. "Hi, David, come on in," she chirped. "You're early, aren't you? Kit mentioned seven-thirty." Joyce Barnes—or Burns, he could never remember which—was a lanky blonde with an unstylish bouffant hairdo.

She wore thick orange lipstick and false eyelashes that never seemed to be quite in place.

"I said, come on in," she said, her voice high, a little shrill. "I can't help you. I just did my nails. Like?" She held out her hands, spreading her fingers in the air. He had never seen such long nails. She blew on them. "The stuff's called Pink Passion or something, can you believe it? Actually, the nails are fake. I bite mine to the quick."

He followed Joyce into the room. "Is Kit ready?"

"Ready? Are you kidding me? You could get here an hour late and you'd still have to wait. She just got out of the shower."

David heard Kit's voice coming from another room. "Is that you, David? Be with you in a minute. Keep him entertained, Joyce."

"You want a beer?" asked Joyce, turning toward the kitchen.

"No, no thanks."

"No? Okay, I'll skip it, too. I don't need it, anyway. Too many calories."

David let the girl's words rush somewhere over his head. People like Joyce irritated him. She was a flurry of nervous energy, constantly waving her arms around absurdly. He didn't attempt to make sense of this girl. Was there anything real beneath her jangly, brash, agitated exterior? He recalled that Kit had said Joyce was a receptionist somewhere. He couldn't imagine where.

She was bubbling on about something, a movie she and Kit had seen, somebody in the movie she especially liked. Automatically David smiled or nodded or shook his head when he thought it was expected of him. He was polite. Certainly he could be polite.

But he wished Kit would hurry. He realized now that he should have walked around the block or stopped for coffee somewhere. Anything to kill time. Just to be some place where he didn't have to listen to this motormouth.

"Sit down, David, come on. For heaven's sake, relax," said Joyce cheerfully, as if the idea of sitting down had sprung upon her unexpectedly. "Don't wait for me to think of it," she said, laughing. She sat down on the couch and patted a space beside her, coaxing him. "You like the news, don't you?" She nodded toward the TV. "The color's not right, do you notice it? The faces are too yellow. Do you know anything about televisions?"

"No," he said vaguely, sitting down where Joyce indicated. He was having a difficult time focusing his thoughts on what she was saying. The news? Sure, he liked the news. No, he knew very little about television sets.

"I was watching the eyewitness news earlier tonight, and they were interviewing the president. He's really cute, don't you think? I just like to watch him. I don't pay much attention to what he says. I mean, who can understand all this political stuff anyway, right?"

"I'm not much into politics," he said, thinking of something else.

"Oh, I know what you mean," she agreed brightly. "There are so many other things to think about. Like parties. And clothes. And guys! Of course, for you it's girls. I should say *one girl,* right? Say, you sure you don't want some beer? We got pretzels, too."

He came back to himself, forgetting whatever it was he was thinking of. "Joyce, really, nothing for me," he said, trying to convince her. "Kit and I will be eating out."

"Oh, yeah, sure," she said. She seemed distracted now. "You don't mind if I smoke, do you?" she asked. She looked at him blankly, a little perturbed perhaps, and asked, "Have you got a cigarette on you? I'm all out."

"No, I don't."

She shrugged. "Oh, well, that's okay. This girl at work calls them 'cancer sticks.' She says I smoke too much. So I die young. So what? No one lives forever, I say."

David smiled. "I don't know about that...."

"Say, I'm going out to dinner tonight, too, believe it or not," said Joyce. She gave her nails an appraising look. "This guy I'm dating works the night shift, but he's off early tonight. He parks cars at this restaurant in Torrance." David watched as Joyce carefully inspected one long, polished nail. "Wow! Almost lost it," she said, sighing with something like relief. "Nothing worse than a chipped nail!"

Kit finally came breezing into the room, smelling of dusting powder and expensive perfume. Her makeup and hair were flawless, and she wore a knit suit, scarlet-red, with a long blazer and short skirt.

David had always thought her appearance attractive—even glamorous. But tonight for some reason he felt her outfit and makeup looked a bit...extreme. Even false. She was trying hard and it showed.

David slipped her supple black lambskin coat around her shoulders and quickly guided her out the door. With a practiced gallantry, he helped her into the passenger seat of his red sports car, then walked around and climbed in on his side, fastening his seat belt.

He looked at Kit and wondered suddenly what to say. There were remnants of feeling for her still inside him, vague memories now. But with gratitude and relief he realized he'd lost a certain attraction to her, and felt no impulse to kiss her cheek, or take her face, her hand. This was the beginning of something new—or more accurately, the end of something old, he realized.

He was not sure what the purpose of this evening was. He would tell Kit of the change within him; he wanted to share this new joy with her. And he would have to tell her it was over between them, this thing that had never really begun.

"Hungry?" he asked, working with his keys, pushing the proper key into the ignition.

"I guess so, yeah. How about you?"

"Sure, famished," he said. What kind of inane conversation was this? He started the car and pulled out into the street.

"It's been a long time," she said lightly, but he knew the subtext of her meaning. *We had something going and you dropped the ball. What happened?*

"Yes, it has been a long time," he agreed with a slight nod of the head, not looking her way. He steered through heavy traffic and finally entered a freeway on-ramp. "How are things at work?" he asked. Work was a fairly harmless topic, although it hadn't been for a few weeks after he lost his job.

"Work's all right, I guess. There's really not much going on. We lost out on another government contract and laid off a few more guys in the shop. We scratch around for things to do, really." She shifted in the seat, turning slightly so that she could look at him. "How about you, David?" she said. "Have you found anything yet?"

"A job? No, nothing yet. I've contacted some agencies back East, and, of course, I've made the rounds out here—but you know how things are in aerospace in Southern California right now."

"I know," she said solemnly. "It's a real bummer, isn't it?"

"Well..." He hesitated. "At least some things in my life are on the upswing."

She gave him a penetrating glance. "You mean your wife?"

"Oh, no. I don't mean Rachel. There's nothing new there." He smiled briefly at her.

"If you weren't talking about your wife, what did you mean about things being on the upswing?" A note of impatience colored her voice.

He stalled. "Well, it's just—things are getting better."

"You're sounding awfully mysterious, David."

"I'm really not trying to."

"Okay, in what way are things better?"

"That's what I want to talk to you about. I thought we could talk over dinner."

"Why dinner? Why not now? Why not tell me now?" she asked, teasing gently, prodding him.

"I thought we could go to that Mexican restaurant on Atlantic. We went there once before, remember?"

She shrugged. "All right."

"That is, if you're hungry for Mexican food...."

"Sure, fine."

"They have great guacamole salad, remember?"

"David, don't put me off," Kit insisted. "I don't like it. Why can't we talk right now?"

He hesitated. "Maybe you won't want to go out to dinner with me after we talk," he said pleasantly, testing her.

"Try me," she said.

"Okay, Kit. Here it is," he replied, steadying his voice, his fingers tapping the steering wheel. "Tonight is sort of a goodbye for us."

"Goodbye?" She looked stricken. "We've hardly said hello," she barely whispered.

"I know. I've led you on, and I—"

"No, I knew—we both knew what we were getting into."

"But it was wrong, Kit. The last thing I want to do is hurt you."

"Hurt me? Don't worry about me. I'm a big girl. I can take care of myself."

"Kit, we can't see each other anymore."

She looked straight ahead and thrust out her chin. "All right."

He stared at her. "*All right?* I don't understand."

"I knew this was coming, David," she said with exaggerated nonchalance. "It just figured. In my head, I already knew."

David felt baffled, a little put down. He pulled off the road into a supermarket parking lot and turned off the engine. "How did you know, Kit? I mean, *I* didn't even know."

Kit's voice was plain now, matter-of-fact. "You kept me at arm's length, David. You wouldn't get involved. Not romantically, anyway. We were never really more than friends. I thought after you left your wife, we might be able to connect, you know, on a serious level. But your heart was never in it."

"I did care, Kit. You know I did."

"Really? From the moment you found out your wife was pregnant, you changed. You started pulling away from me. Any other man would have seized the opportunities I gave you. But we never had a chance, did we? Because you never stopped loving your wife. I knew it. I had it figured. I'm not surprised."

David's mouth felt dry, his lips stiff. He ran his moist palm over the leather-wrapped steering wheel. How could he make her understand what he himself couldn't fully comprehend? "It wasn't like that, Kit. I cared about you. I thought we had something special. But I told you from the start I couldn't get seriously involved until I could commit myself, until I knew where I was going."

"And you know now?"

"Yes, I do," he said with a ragged sigh. This wasn't easy. He'd never been good at pouring out his guts. "I've finally made a—a commitment, Kit."

Her tone was breezy, biting. "And this wonderful new commitment of yours doesn't include me at all, does it, David." This was not a question but a statement.

"Not the way you think, not the way we hoped," he conceded. "There can't be anything between us, Kit, because the whole direction of my life has changed."

"Hey, that's heady stuff, David," she said with a hint of sarcasm.

"Yeah, it is heady. I just wish I could make you understand."

She gave him a bemused look. "Give it a shot. I'm

listening. You're not trying to tell me there's someone else, are you—besides your wife?"

He smiled, relaxing a little. "Actually, Kit, yes," he said gently. "In a way there is someone else. I don't want to spout platitudes. That's not my style, believe me. Well, you know me. I don't have to tell you how I am."

"No, I know you pretty well. Not as well as I'd hoped, of course."

"Something happened to me, Kit. Something I never expected. And I'm having a hard time figuring how to tell you about it."

Her eyes narrowed suspiciously. "What do you mean?"

"I can't put words around it, Kit. I can't give it a definition. There's no label for it. All I can say is, Jesus Christ isn't just a word to me anymore. He's a living person, and He's done something for me I can't begin to understand. Kit, it's unreal. It's like falling in love...like being set free."

"Oh, terrific. It's a God thing. Is that it? You've joined Rachel's church? You're converting to her religion?"

David shook his head, scouring his mind for the right words. "No, I'm not just talking about religion here. It's so much more than that. I'm talking about being committed to a person, to God Himself, personally. I know this will blow your mind—it blows mine—but I've come to know Jesus Christ. How can I explain it to you, Kit? He's real, and He loves me. And He loves you."

"Oh, man, this *is* a church thing. I knew it!"

"No, Kit, it's—it's a relationship, a commitment. It's what I was looking for all along and just never knew it." He paused a moment. "As far as church is concerned, I haven't thought yet about a church. But I suppose now I should...."

Kit fingered the collar of her lambskin coat. "David, you don't have to get into this...." Her voice trailed off.

David flashed a hapless grin. "I don't know what to say to convince you, Kit. It's as if I've been going in circles all my life, like a whirling dervish or something, and now for the first time I've stopped, and I can see things clearly. I mean, real things. And it's beautiful."

"That's nice, David, for *you.*" Kit sounded unconvinced, detached, her voice flat. She was pulling away, erecting a barrier between them.

"I'd like to tell you more about it, Kit," he said tentatively.

"No, David. I get the message." She folded her arms against her chest and stared out the windshield as if something else, far away, had attracted her attention. "I don't mind. I understand. Sort of. I don't get the religion thing. But I expected the rest. I took a chance and lost. It really doesn't matter. I see to it that nothing matters too much."

David lifted his hand to touch her arm, then withdrew it. "I'm sorry, Kit. I'm really sorry." He knew for a fact: Only the Spirit of God could reach Kit Kincaid. "I just wish there was something more I could do."

Kit laughed, a brilliant, excited laugh. "David," she said brightly, "there is. I'm starved, really I am. Let's get back on the road and find that fabulous restaurant, okay? We'll celebrate...and then say goodbye."

Chapter Fifteen

Often lately Rachel found herself thinking, *What does a woman do when her husband goes away and does not come back? How does she feel, knowing he's involved with another woman?* Left alone with her thoughts, for days and months Rachel fell into a rut thinking nothing existed, not even her own body, or her unborn child, or her own soul. She lost touch with God, although she tried again and again to reach God, to make Him real.

Then one day David phoned and wanted to talk with her—not with Brian, their son, but with her. He had something very important to tell her. Could he come to see her?

She marveled at the feeling—the silent, secret, remote joy, the slivers of excitement and growing anticipation—as she replaced the telephone receiver into its cradle. Like a woman in a dream, she went straight to her room and changed into a favorite dress, freshened her face and brushed her hair. She inspected her image in the mirror, scrutinizing, slightly critical of the swelling of her body, the heaviness. Yet she was somehow pleased. She stared at herself in the glass—her eyes, her brows, her slender neck—and she wondered what it meant. She had been trying too hard, too long, to make sense of her life. She had known the answers once; obviously she had. Where were the answers now?

Her husband would be here to see her. At any moment he would arrive. He had something to say. Perhaps she would find answers in his words. Perhaps her husband would come with words to make things real.

The doorbell rang. Once. Twice. Rachel went to answer it, breathless with hurrying, breathless with expectancy. What did she expect? What could David possibly have to say that would make any difference now? Was it too late for words?

She opened the door.

"Hello, Rachel." David stood, smiling, one hand on the door frame, the other offering her a bouquet of red roses in an apparent gesture of conciliation. He looked as handsome as she'd ever seen him, tall, tanned and robust in a hunter green, stonewashed shirt and casual slacks. "I hope I'm not too early."

"No, of course not. I told you to come right over. Come in." She directed him inside and invited him to sit down. It was like a ritual, an exercise in formality. He chose his old recliner; she took the sofa. She was wearing a cranberry baby-doll dress with a scoop neckline. It was her only dress roomy enough to accommodate her blossoming figure. For a fleeting moment she wished she still had the svelte body David had always admired. She could imagine him mentally comparing her bulky shape with Kit's willowy contours.

"How have you been feeling, Rae?" he asked, sitting forward, rubbing his hands together.

"Not too bad," she said, her voice light.

"And the pregnancy? Everything okay?"

She nodded. "I'm awfully tired lately, but the doctor says that's normal, with the baby due in six weeks."

"Just six weeks! That's hard to believe."

"It feels like forever. The baby must weigh a ton, he's so heavy. You probably noticed, I waddle now instead of walk." She smiled slightly, averting her eyes, feeling somehow embarrassed.

David's eyes shone with tenderness. "No, Rae. You still walk with the grace of a Madonna. You look lovely. Must be that healthy glow of motherhood."

"I don't see it...but thank you." She could tell David was nervous, the way he massaged his knuckles, kneading each one with his thumb. He had something important to say, something to tell her that would change their lives forever. She sensed it, felt it at the very marrow of her bones. Maybe he had come to ask for a divorce. Maybe he would tell her he was marrying Kit.

"Listen, Rachel," he said in a tentative voice, "we haven't talked much about the baby, about the baby's birth. Are you planning on natural childbirth?"

She drew in a deep breath. "I'm not sure. You remember my experience with Brian."

David's mouth tightened. "He was breech. It was a long, hard delivery. I'd never seen anyone so brave as you."

"These days I don't feel so brave."

"This time may not be as bad. You've been through it before. You know what to expect."

"And that should make it easier? In some ways it was easier not knowing what was coming." As if to punctuate her remark, the baby kicked her hard under her ribs, stealing her breath momentarily.

David sat forward, concern written on his face. "What is it? Are you okay?"

She nodded. "The baby just gave me one swift kick."

"Must be a boy." David's expression softened. "I remember how we used to feel Brian moving in your tummy. He used to squirm around like a little acrobat. Arching his back, turning somersaults, stretching his legs. We used to lie there at night watching your belly rise and fall in little hills and valleys. We were laughing at Brian's antics before we even laid eyes on him."

"I remember," said Rachel softly.

David's voice broke. "I've never felt this baby."

Rachel smiled. "You can, if you like. He's kicking right now."

David slipped out of his chair and knelt beside Rachel. Gingerly he placed his hand on her abdomen. She guided his hand to the right spot. "Feel it?"

He broke into a grin. "Do I ever. This little tyke is all over the place. How do you get any rest, Rae, with this little tiger kicking up a storm?"

She laughed. "I don't. I sneak naps when he's sleeping."

"It's incredible. He's really there, isn't he? My son or daughter?"

"In six weeks he'll really be here, in every way.

And then no one will get any rest. I really don't know if I'm ready for it."

Impulsively David laid his cheek against Rachel's belly and listened. "Our baby says to tell Mommy it won't be so bad this time. He's going to be a perfect baby."

"Sure, I've heard that before." Her hand moved instinctively to David's tousled hair. It had been ages since he'd rested his head in her lap. She wanted desperately to hold him against her and feel his loving warmth. Was it possible he wanted that closeness as much as she?

Gently, through the folds of her rayon dress, he kissed the spot where the baby moved. "I love you, little guy," he whispered.

Rachel flinched, a pang of disappointment wrenching her chest. Suddenly she understood. She wasn't the one he loved; it was their baby. David had to be close to her to get to the baby. She removed her fingers from his hair and shifted her weight. "That's enough, David. I'm tired."

He stood and returned to the recliner. "I'm sorry, Rachel. It's just—for the first time this baby is starting to be real to me." He sighed. "Listen, I want to be there for you when the time comes."

"Be there?"

"For the baby's birth. If that means I need to take some classes—"

"You mean Lamaze?"

"Whatever they call them, sure."

"You're saying you want to be my coach?"

"Is that what they call it? Yeah, your coach. Whatever."

She moved her hands over her abdomen. "I've already asked Marlene."

"Marlene? Why would you ask her?"

"She's my best friend."

David's voice tightened. "I have a right to be there, Rachel. It's my baby."

She stared at him with fire in her eyes. "You gave up your rights when you walked out on me."

Ruefully he said, "As I recall, you're the one who sent me packing."

"And you're the one who went looking for love in all the wrong places."

David shook his head. "Maybe I shouldn't have come."

"Then why did you?" she asked in a small voice.

"I just wanted to talk. I didn't come to upset you."

"But you did anyway."

They were both silent for several moments. Rachel wished David would just get up and go. It was too painful having him so near and yet so far away. Didn't he realize what his presence did to her, bringing back all the memories of their closeness and reminding her of what she no longer had?

In a quiet, guarded voice, David asked, "How's Brian?"

"All right." She hesitated. "He's having problems in school."

David's face registered surprise. "What kind of problems?"

"Nothing serious. Mainly his grades. He's been getting C's and D's."

"He always got A's and B's before."

"Yes, something's wrong," she admitted. Her voice felt strangled. Her emotions were too near the surface—her yearnings for David, her worries about Brian. Was she going to cry? "I can't reach our son anymore, David. I can't say anything to him. He's changed so much since you went away."

"I didn't realize it was that bad."

She searched his eyes. "Haven't you noticed a difference in him?"

David's brows lowered. "Yes, I suppose I have, but he's always cheerful when we go out. He always seems to enjoy being with me. I hoped I was only imagining a change."

Rachel drew in a ragged breath. "Well, Brian just sulks around me. He has nothing to say. He hangs around with Ronnie Mayhew and won't tell me what they do. I can hardly get him to go to church anymore."

"You mean, he's stopped going to church?"

"Practically. I don't know whether to twist his arm or just give in and leave him home."

David straightened his shoulders. "Listen, Rachel, that's one of the things I came to talk to you about."

"You mean Brian?"

"Yes, Brian, too, but—"

"About Brian going to church?" she asked, puzzled.

"No. I mean, we will have to discuss Brian and church, but I wanted to talk about something else."

"What, David?"

"Something having to do with church."

"I don't understand. You sounded so urgent on the phone."

David stood and walked to the window. "Rachel, I went to see your pastor last week."

She studied the solid contour of his back. "Pastor Emrick?"

"We had a long talk. We talked for a whole evening."

"Why did you go see Pastor Emrick?"

"I was desperate, Rachel. You know I lost my job."

"Yes, Brian told me. I thought I'd hear it directly from you, but you were obviously avoiding me."

"I know. I wanted to tell you, but I just couldn't bring myself to face you. It seemed like there was nothing left." He turned and looked at her, apparently trying to read her expression. "I suppose Marlene told you how I barged in on her…very angry."

Rachel looked away. "Yes, she told me."

"I'm afraid I really frightened her. She told me to go see your pastor. I thought of what she said a few weeks later and decided to do it. I didn't know what else to do. I was at the end of my rope."

"I'm sorry, David. I didn't realize—"

"It's all right," he said quickly. "I guess I had to hit rock bottom before I was ready to look for an answer outside myself."

She looked up at him. "What happened?"

He came back and sat down. "Pastor Emrick helped me see things in a new light."

"What things?"

David shifted his position. "He made me see how all the evils of this world are the result of sin, and sin starts with the individual, with me."

Rachel stared at him, incredulous. "You understand that now?"

"Yes, Pastor Emrick helped me see that Christ paid

the price for my sins. I've been forgiven. The burden is gone."

Rachel tried to focus her eyes on her husband, tried to comprehend him. She could feel David's words dazing her, putting her in a trance. "David," she said, her voice hardly there, "David, you're saying you accepted Christ as your Savior?"

"That's what I'm trying to tell you," he said, his eyes brilliant, jubilant as his voice. "That's what I'm saying, Rachel."

"I prayed for you for so long, I—"

"I know. You were so patient."

"But I wasn't patient."

"I made your life a nightmare. I rejected you because I thought you were rejecting me." His voice softened as he said, "But it will be all right now, Rae."

She studied his features, the intensity in his eyes. "What do you mean, David?"

He reached out and clasped her hands. "I want you to know, Rachel, I've broken off with Kit. Before—last fall—I was searching for something, for some meaning in my life, and I guess I thought Kit held that meaning. Or maybe I'm just using pretty words to excuse my sin, my selfishness, wanting something I had no right to. I don't know. But I was trying to fill a need in my life, an emptiness. Maybe I was really searching for an answer to my own guilt. The point is I know now that Christ is the only answer for a man...for me."

Rachel tried to listen, tried to push the fuzziness out of her head. Who was this man? What did he have to do with her? For months she had tried to expel him from her life, from her emotions. She had nearly convinced herself he was no part of her. She was a whole person, a fulfilled woman, without him. But now, what he was saying at this moment was important, vital, something she had to deal with. Why did she feel so numb? "I can't believe this is you talking, David," she said, shaking her head.

He leaned forward, still holding her hands. His face was flushed, his expression animated. He talked quickly. "For the first time I know where I'm going, Rachel, and I know why God put me here. People spend all their lives looking for answers, and here it is. Here it is all the time!"

She smiled, not looking directly at him but only in his direction. "I used to feel that kind of excitement, that enthusiasm, like you have now. I used to feel that way."

"What do you mean, *used to?*"

"I don't know, David. I can't seem to hold on to that feeling anymore, the joy of being a Christian. I try and try—"

"Oh, baby, have I done this to you, driven you away from the Lord? Did I do this?"

"No, of course not, David. It's just that everything has pulled me down. I seem to struggle with the Lord, trying to get closer to Him."

David moved over to the sofa and sat beside Rachel. She moved slightly, neither accepting nor rejecting his closeness. He touched her face with his hands, gently touching, stroking. She sat immobile, saying nothing, her eyes directed away from him, but she could not move, could not respond. What did he want from her? What did he want her to say? What was wrong, that she could not respond?

"Rachel," he said softly, "I want you back. I want to come home. I want us together again."

She said nothing; her eyes remained focused somewhere else, on some indefinite spot. Her thoughts were locked within her. She sat very still.

"Did you hear me, Rachel? I want us together again. Do you understand?"

"Yes, I hear you, I hear you," she said, her voice echoing mechanically. "I don't know what to say. I need time. I can't take all of this in at once. Can you understand? I'm happy for you, but I need time."

"Yes, of course," David said slowly. There was a note of dejection in his voice and a look of disappointment etched in the lines of his face. He seemed perplexed, confused. "I won't push you, Rae. I won't push you," he said, trying to reassure her.

But Rachel wasn't ready to listen.

Chapter Sixteen

Rachel was in no mood to go shopping, but she allowed herself to be talked into it. Marlene was an excellent persuader. It was a warm Saturday morning. Marlene's favorite clothing store at the mall was having a spring sale or pre-Easter sale or perhaps just an end-of-winter sale. Who knew? It was a sale.

Neatly lettered posterboard signs adorned the windows and the counters. In the yardage department, signs glittered in slick, bright yellows and oranges.

Marlene couldn't quite make up her mind whether she wanted to purchase a new dress or buy some material to make her own. Obligingly, Rachel followed her through the yardage department, chatting amiably as they inspected rolls and rolls of material.

Later, as Rachel moved from chair to chair or rested against the counter, Marlene browsed through the endless racks of women's dresses, occasionally offering her opinion or randomly checking a price tag. "Honey," she said, shaking her head, "there's no way either one of us can fit into these dresses!"

Marlene was right. Since tents and muumuus were not in style, Rachel couldn't possibly squeeze herself into any of these delicate, clinging outfits.

"Maybe we should try the maternity department," Marlene suggested.

Rachel waved her off, laughing. "I'm not going to spend fifty dollars for a dress I can wear only another month or so."

"Well, I wouldn't be putting out any money for a dress right now if it weren't such a special occasion," said Marlene eagerly, her fingers breezing through a rack of colorful plus-size garments.

Rachel smiled and said nothing, knowing Marlene wanted to tell her again what she had already told her three times this morning.

"He called and I didn't even know who it was at first," Marlene said breathlessly. "I thought maybe it was my boss calling to tell me he had to go out of town or something. I couldn't believe it was Mr. Timmons. I mean Stan. He said I should call him Stan, or Stanley, if I want. Some people call him Stan, some call him Stanley. Well, I mean, it doesn't matter, but there he was, Mr. Timmons—Stan—on the phone asking me to have dinner with him. Just like that. I couldn't believe it."

"Did he say how he happened to call?" asked Rachel. There was another chair nearby so she sat down, relieved to be off her feet again.

"He just said he thought it was time for us to get better acquainted. You know how I've dreamed of this, Rachel."

"Dreamed?" she teased. "I thought you'd call it an answer to prayer."

"It is," Marlene agreed happily. She removed a

dress from the rack—a blue jersey knit dress with a ruffled neckline—and inspected the price tag. "Of course," she added slyly, "I'm happy about something else, too."

"What do you mean?" Rachel asked with a note of caution.

"You know what I mean," said Marlene, deliberately avoiding Rachel's gaze, focusing her attention instead on the garment in her hands. "Say, do you like this one? It's size fourteen. Bet I couldn't get into it, though."

"It's a perfect shade of blue for you. Why don't you try it on?" Rachel urged. "So what else are you happy about?"

Marlene ignored her. "I've been gaining lately, I'm sure I have." She held the knit dress up and scrutinized her image in the mirror. "I bet I'm past size sixteen now," she lamented.

"Well, try it on and see."

Marlene hesitated, glancing shrewdly at Rachel. "What I meant before was, I think it's tremendous what's happened to David."

Rachel nodded. "Yes, it is."

"You don't sound exactly euphoric about it."

"I'm happy for him, Marlene. Of course I'm happy."

"Then what's the matter?"

Rachel shrugged. "He wants to come back home now."

Marlene hung the knit dress back on the rack and selected a black chemise with a jewel neckline. Size sixteen. "What's wrong with him coming home, honey? I figured you'd be shouting for joy."

"Maybe once I would have, but so much has happened.... I don't know if I can change my feelings overnight, just like that.''

''Don't you love him anymore?''

Rachel's voice wavered. ''I don't know how I feel, Marlene. I've tried for so many months to get him out of my mind, out of my heart. And just when I thought I'd succeeded, he comes waltzing back and wants to pick up where we left off, as if everything were perfectly fine. I can't do that, Marlene.''

Marlene laughed. ''He couldn't do much waltzing with you right now.''

''I suppose he could tell by my silence I wasn't ready to pick up the pieces.''

Marlene's usually bubbly expression turned solemn. ''Be sure you know what you're doing, honey. Don't throw something precious away just because you're angry with your man.''

Rachel looked away. ''Don't I have a right to be angry?''

Marlene thought a moment. ''I'm afraid sometimes our rights get in the way of what's right.''

Rachel looked helplessly at Marlene. ''I don't know what's right anymore. A part of my heart tells me David and I should get back together, but another part tells me I don't feel the same about him anymore.''

Marlene reached out and smoothed Rachel's hair. ''That's because you're still hurting, baby.''

Rachel stiffened. ''Why wouldn't I be? These last few months have been terrible. I didn't know it could be so bad.''

''Then you do still love David?''

Tears glazed Rachel's eyes. ''I suppose I do. But, Marlene, it's not a fresh, pure love anymore. It's all tarnished and marred. There are so many other things besides love mixed into my feelings now. I don't know if I can trust David anymore. And, to be honest, I resent him. I resent everything he's done to me. I know it's a sin, but that's how I feel."

Marlene hung the chemise over her arm and reached for a navy patchwork-print dress with an empire waist. "What do you think, Rachel?"

"The pattern's too busy."

"You're right. I'd better stick with the chemise." Marlene's voice grew confidential. "You know David's going to church now, don't you?"

"Yes, I saw him last Sunday."

"Really? Did you talk?"

"We didn't say much."

"But he must have said something. I hear that certain lilt in your voice."

Rachel forced herself to sound nonchalant. "He asked me if I'd go out with him sometime."

"For a date?"

"Yes, a date." Rachel let a smile escape. "Kind of funny, huh? Eight months pregnant and dating your own husband?"

"I'd say it's a good start. When are you going out?"

"Did I say I'd accepted?"

"If you know what's good for you, gal, you will!"

"Okay, I accepted. I felt like a silly schoolgirl. And here I am big as a house. What's wrong with this picture, Marlene? It's crazy!"

"The picture looks perfect to me—you and David having a fresh start. So when's the big date?"

"Next Friday night. I don't know what we'll do."

"I know what you should do," declared Marlene. "You should give your husband another chance."

Rachel stood and browsed without interest through a rack of sale merchandise. "I don't know if I can, Marlene. But I'm willing to let the Lord change my attitudes. I want you to know that."

"I'm glad, Rachel." Marlene turned to the floor-length mirror and held the chemise up to herself again. "When the two of you get back together, the Lord will really bless you. Now, if you'll hold my purse for me, I'll go see if I can struggle into this luscious chemise."

After making their purchases, Rachel and Marlene stopped for lunch at a nearby café and ordered chicken salad sandwiches and iced tea. Marlene had chocolate pie for dessert; Rachel had a small dish of vanilla ice cream.

"I shouldn't eat this pie," mused Marlene, opening her mouth for another forkful. "That dress barely fit me as it is."

"Nonsense, it fit you perfectly," Rachel said, smiling.

Marlene returned a long, appraising look. "I think I've run you ragged today, hon. How do you feel? You look tired."

"I am. The least little thing makes me tired now. But I enjoyed today, I really did."

"That's good, but I'm taking you right home. I want you to go to bed and take a nap for the rest of the afternoon."

"We'll see," said Rachel. "But I'm really all right."

"No, you're not. A fool could see how exhausted

you are. Is it the baby? Are you having any problems?''

''Just some false labor pains. They don't hurt, but they're annoying.''

Marlene's brows shot up. ''False labor? Sounds serious to me.''

Rachel put her hands on her bountiful middle. ''It's a tightening, a hardness of the muscles right here. I remember feeling this way with Brian a few weeks before he was born.''

''Oh, my goodness!'' Marlene clasped her hands to her bosom. ''Don't you dare have that baby right here, girl!''

Rachel laughed so hard it hurt. ''I promise I won't.''

''You can't be sure. I never had a baby, but I had this aunt who had this tiny little backache and the next thing you know—''

''Marlene, believe me, the baby isn't due for five or six weeks yet. The doctor said this is normal. The muscles are just contracting to get in practice for the big day. Rehearsing, you know?''

They both laughed. ''I'm just glad you're the one having the baby,'' said Marlene, scraping the last crumbs of pie from her plate.

''I'm trying to be prepared. I even bought some books.''

''Books?''

''On natural childbirth, things like that. I was scared to death when I had Brian. I didn't know anything. I want to be ready this time.''

''What can a book tell you about having a baby?''

''There's a lot the mother can do to prepare herself—exercises and things.''

"Exercises?"

"Sure. Have you ever heard of 'psychoprophylaxis'?"

"Heard of it? I can't even say it."

Rachel laughed. "It means preparing a woman psychologically and physically for childbirth. Surely you've heard of the Lamaze method, with breathing exercises and all."

"Lordy, I can't imagine it!"

Rachel lowered her voice. "I've got a confession to make, Marlene. I signed up for a natural childbirth class."

"Gal, if it were me going into labor, I'd tell them to put me out until it's all over with. I wouldn't want to know a thing."

"Not me," said Rachel. "I can't stand feeling helpless, out of control. I don't want it to be like last time, being so scared, not knowing what's about to happen. I couldn't go through that again."

"Well, I admire your determination," said Marlene.

"But I haven't told you the rest of my confession," said Rachel.

"There's more?"

Rachel stifled a whimsical smile. "I lied to David."

"Lied? No!"

"I didn't mean to. He asked about Lamaze classes, and I told him you're going to be my coach."

Marlene clasped her hands to her mouth. "Me? Your coach? Honey, I'd go to the ends of the earth for our friendship, but no way I'll be there when that baby pops out!"

"I know, but please don't tell David that. Let it be our little secret, okay?"

Marlene started to laugh giddily. "Can you imagine me being your coach? I'd have to do it blindfolded, from the sidelines, or maybe by remote control!" She assumed the exaggerated voice of a sportscaster. "Okay, folks, that little one's coming down the home stretch. He's rounding the bend. Crossing the finish line. Where's that doc? We need a wide receiver. Rachel's going to deliver this one to the outfield!"

Rachel was laughing now, too. "Thank heavens you're not my coach!"

Marlene switched to a Southern accent. "I don't know nothin' about birthing babies. Or running races or passing footballs!"

They were both in hysterics now. The more they tried to stifle their laughter, the louder and more convulsive it became, until it erupted in gales. The merriment was contagious. Several patrons at nearby tables had turned and looked their way and were chuckling, too. When the baby finally jabbed her ribs in protest, Rachel managed to quench her levity with a glass of water.

"Well, laughter's good medicine," said Marlene, catching her breath.

Rachel wiped tears from her eyes. "I laughed so hard, the baby has hiccups. Can you believe that?"

"You're kidding me."

"No, I'm not. Really, hiccups. I can feel them. Rhythmic little beats."

Marlene still looked dubious. "Really? A little rat-a-tat in the tummy, huh? Maybe this kid's going to be a drummer. Tell him to take it easy with the drumsticks in that cramped little condo of his.''

They both laughed again. It seemed like ages since Rachel had surrendered herself to such delicious, refreshing hilarity.

The phone was ringing when Rachel got home. She fumbled with her key and finally got the door open, but Brian was there and already had the phone. ''It's for me,'' he said quickly and turned his back to talk, shutting her out.

Rachel dragged herself wearily to the bedroom, kicked off her shoes, wriggled out of her dress and slipped into a comfy terry-cloth robe. Her feet were swollen and her legs ached. She needed to rest, take a nap.

Then she thought about dinner. She had better put out something to thaw, pork chops, perhaps. Brian liked pork chops. She started for the kitchen, where she could hear Brian still talking on the phone. A menacing sound in his tone made her stop and listen. Alarm quickened her pulse. Her skin felt prickly and cold.

''I told you, nobody's going to find it,'' he said, his voice a rough whisper. ''I got it taken care of, man. It's okay.''

When Brian hung up the phone, his face looked white and drawn, older than his years. There was something behind his expression, a cryptic message Rachel couldn't read. When he saw her looking at him, he smiled faintly and the dark look vanished; he was just Brian again.

''How you feeling, Mom?'' He sounded solicitous, but he didn't wait for her answer. He pulled on his leather jacket and headed for the door. "Anything you need, Mom? I gotta go out. Got things to do."

"Wait, Brian," she cried as he bolted out the door. "Where are you going? How long will you be gone?"

"To Ronnie's," he called back as he ran across the yard to his bike. "School project. Due Monday."

"Be home early!" she shouted after him. But already he was pedaling off into the hazy, salmon pink sunset.

She had lost control of Brian. When had it happened? What was happening to her son? To her?

Too tense to relax, Rachel went back to her room and lay down on the bed. Something was wrong; she knew it. She tried to sleep, but sleep was elusive now. Ideas, random thoughts bombarded her mind, swirled in her head. Why couldn't she rest? Something was wrong with Brian. Something in his expression froze inside her, leaving her cold and afraid. When he'd been talking to her, his voice had been smooth and bright as crystal, but on the phone it had been sharp and jagged as splintered glass.

Who had he been talking to? Ronnie? Probably. What were they saying? Something about hiding something—no, something about no one finding it. What? What would no one find? What was he hiding? Why would Brian hide something?

Brian is in trouble! Rachel sat up, startled. Yes, that was it. Brian was in serious trouble. Fighting waves of anxiety, Rachel got up and padded to her son's room, as if seeing everything in its place might reassure her.

What would a young boy hide from people? Rachel wondered. From his parents? His mother? What would he feel the need to hide? A *Playboy* centerfold? Cigarettes? Things stolen from some store?

Guardedly she looked around Brian's room. Everything was neat and in order, nothing out of place. But something was hidden here, cached away; it must be here, whatever it was. Where else but here in Brian's room, his world, where he kept his treasures?

She could begin by searching; she could go through the whole room, turning things upside down, until she found the secret, the thing that made Brian a puzzle to her now. If she chose, she could spend hours looking for clues to this boy she no longer understood.

Or could she? Rachel had always trusted Brian. His things belonged to him, were his private affair. She had never invaded that privacy; she had always respected his rights.

But there was something here.

Nobody's going to find it, he had said. She had heard him say it.

Rachel went to Brian's bureau and eased open a drawer. Each week she went to this bureau and opened the drawers, putting away clean clothes—socks, underwear, sweaters, shirts. She made nice, orderly piles of Brian's clothing, smoothing out wrinkles, item after item in neat stacks. She knew these drawers and kept them in good order. There could be nothing here, nothing to suspect.

But there was the bottom drawer—Brian's junk drawer—which she had no reason to keep in order, no reason to notice at all. It was full of the things Brian collected, odds and ends, she supposed. Once he had kept toy trucks and plastic soldiers and bits and pieces of broken games there, in that bottom drawer that was lowest and most accessible to a child. Now, who knew what was there?

She leaned down awkwardly, and finally had to get on her knees to open the drawer. She would look here quickly and then that was it. Brian's secrets were his own. She would look nowhere else, but this one drawer just might offer a clue.

The drawer was a shambles, a vast disarray of random articles—stacks of baseball cards, string, old schoolwork, photographs of school friends, a rock collection from Big Bear, a tattered book of David's on auto mechanics, a worn cigar box with…

She opened the box.

Cigarettes. She might have known, cigarettes.

No, no, not cigarettes. She looked more closely, bringing the box up to her face. She picked up one long taper, very narrow, thin, and turned it between her fingers. The paper was odd, twisted at the ends. And that sweet, musky smell…

Somehow she knew.

"Oh, God, no," she said, "not marijuana."

She sat on the floor and began to sob. "Dear God, please not Brian! Please, not my son, not Brian!"

Chapter Seventeen

The doorbell rang. Rachel was there immediately, opening the door before the echo of ringing had faded, welcoming David into the room, greeting him formally without a smile. She observed at once the cords of strain in his face. Reading his eyes, she knew he sensed the same painful tension in her.

"David," she said, but her thoughts trailed off like wind.

"Rachel," he said briskly, rubbing his hands together as if they might be numb with cold, although it was not cold outside. "You were right to call me."

"I didn't know what else to do," she replied, hardly more than whispering.

"Brian's smoking pot—that's how it looks?"

She hugged herself, trembling. "I don't know. I think so. I found marijuana in his room, in a cigar box in his drawer. I'm sure it's marijuana."

"Where is it?"

"There." She indicated a box on the coffee table.

David examined the contents painstakingly. The severity of his expression silenced Rachel, although she had a dozen questions to ask him. She waited for him to finish his investigation and turn again to her, and when at last he did, there was a brittleness to his voice. "I was afraid of this...I should have realized—"

"What are we going to do? Brian will be home any time."

"I suppose we should turn this stuff over to the police."

"The police? Turn our own son over to the police? David, no!"

"I didn't say that. I don't mean..."

Rachel sat down, curving her body into the contour of the sofa. She beckoned David to sit down and moved over awkwardly, making room for him. He dropped down beside her heavily, his face blank. Rachel had the impression his mental acuity had been short-circuited. This disturbed her. She needed something from him—strength, good advice, a solution.

"Brian's only thirteen," she said thickly, feeling a vague growing panic inside. "Just a child, David. We've got to help him. We have to do something to help him out of this."

The tendons in David's neck were taut, bulging slightly beneath the skin. "I don't know what to do," he said.

She blinked back tears. "I don't, either."

"I noticed little things about Brian," he said, looking at her imploringly, "but I tried to tell myself they didn't mean anything. What about you, Rachel? You should have noticed any signs that Brian is on drugs."

Rachel stiffened. "I knew his school grades were slipping, things like that," she replied unevenly. "He was gone a lot, you know that. He wouldn't confide in me."

"Did you notice any erratic behavior, mental confusion, extreme moods?"

Rachel shook her head. "I don't think so, David." Her voice was too loud, thin and sharp like steel, like a knife. "I don't think so!"

"Can't you be sure?" he demanded.

"No, no, I can't. I can't think right now. I'm too upset to remember anything."

David pushed the bulk of his frame back into the couch and sighed deeply. Reaching out, he took her hand and gently rubbed his thumb over her delicate fingers. "I'm sorry, Rae. I didn't mean to start in on you," he said softly. "I'm as upset as you are. This thing leaves me cold. I just don't know what to do."

Rachel was aware that David's breathing was labored; he seemed to be fighting to control some secret outrage within himself. She could feel its power surging from his hand into hers, through her. There was a certain strength, a raw-boned courage, in such anger.

With her free hand she touched his arm, his wrist, drew her fingers lightly up along the length of his forearm, aware of the fine layer of hair on the back of his arm and the tanned flesh and solid bone of his wrist. Her touch would be only brief comfort for this tired man, but at least a spontaneous gesture of—what? Affection? Love?

She attempted a smile. "We'll think of something, David, something. Can I get you some coffee?"

"No, no, thanks, Rachel, unless you want some. Have you eaten yet?"

"No, I was going to fix pork chops for dinner, but I got sidetracked. I'm not hungry now."

"You should eat. Something light, a snack. How about some scrambled eggs? I'll fix them for you."

She hesitated only a moment, then nodded.

They went to the kitchen and Rachel sat down at the table while David put a frying pan on the stove. While he melted some butter in the pan, he beat some eggs in a bowl, added a dash of milk and then poured the mixture into the sizzling yellow fat. He stirred it vigorously with a fork until the liquid thickened into fluffy golden mounds.

"It helps to be doing something," Rachel said. She rose and took plates from the cupboard and some silverware from a drawer. He served the eggs, poured two glasses of milk and sat down beside Rachel.

"Looks great," she said.

"Thanks," David replied. "Feel any better?"

"Yes, thanks. Not quite so strung out," Rachel said.

He reached across the table and touched her hand. "Good."

She slipped her hand easily into his. "Before you arrived, David, I was trying to think what I know about drugs, and, you know, I really couldn't think of much. I've read magazine articles, newspaper stories, and even seen a few TV specials, but outside of that, what do I know? What do I know about real people needing drugs or playing around with narcotics? It doesn't make any sense to me, David. I can't relate to it. So how can I talk to Brian?"

"I don't know, Rachel."

"I keep saying there has to be a logical explanation for this, something to explain it away so it will be as if I never found that cigar box, as if there were nothing to find."

"It's not like that," replied David. "It did happen. Something's going on and we have to find out what it is."

"Will he tell us?"

"I hope so, Rachel. I sure hope so."

For a few moments they lapsed into silence and ate eagerly, as if they had underestimated their hunger. When David finished his eggs, he sat back and looked thoughtfully at his wife. "You know, Rachel, when it comes right down to it, when something like this hits you where you live, all of your objectivity goes right out the window and you're just as vulnerable, just as open to hurt as the next guy."

"You feel that way, too?" Rachel asked, vaguely surprised. "I hadn't thought of you being hurt. Hurt implies being needy, vulnerable—"

"It implies caring," corrected David.

Rachel nodded. "Yes, yes, you're right, of course."

"But I also feel guilty, Rae."

"Guilty? Why?"

David's voice was husky. "I fought you and Brian so much. I rejected your faith, ridiculed you."

"It wasn't just you, David. It was everything. Me, Brian, the whole situation. We all contributed. And you weren't a Christian. You didn't realize—"

"That's no excuse."

"No, it's not, but I feel guilty sometimes, too."

"You? What did you do?"

Rachel toyed with her fork, tracing the flower design on her plate. "I don't know if I can explain, David. It's just that I haven't let the Lord have control of me for a long time. For months I've been wrapped up in my own little world of resentment and bitterness. I admit, David, I've been bitter against you."

"You had every reason to be."

"But I don't want to feel that way anymore. I'm sorry, David. I was struggling with the Lord to get closer to Him, wanting His closeness without submitting to His will. Does that make sense?"

"I think so. I think I understand."

"I don't want it to be that way anymore. I want God to forgive the resentment and take it away. But I think I've already hurt Brian. That's what scares me."

"God is fair, Rachel. We have to trust Him. The only thing I know to do is to trust Him with this."

"Yes, you're right." Rachel got up from the table and cleared away the plates and glasses. David helped her rinse the dishes and stack them on the counter. They started for the living room but stopped suddenly when they heard the click of the front door. Brian came in, hurrying, his feet moving in quick smooth strides across the carpet. He was whistling something, a familiar tune.

"Brian," said David curtly.

The boy turned abruptly, obviously startled, and stared at them. "Dad," he said, smiling unevenly, sounding breathless, "what are you doing here?"

Chapter Eighteen

Brian's gaze drifted across the room to the cigar box on the table. He shot a comprehending glance at his parents and stormed, "What are you doing getting into my stuff? Who said you could snoop into my things? That's private property, that stuff. It's none of your business!"

"It's my business if you're smoking marijuana," replied David sharply.

"Marijuana? Where'd you get a crazy idea like that?"

"From that box," David answered.

Brian stiffened, throwing back his lean, angular shoulders. "That stuff isn't mine. You should have left it alone. It doesn't belong to me."

"Then whose is it?" asked Rachel, her voice thin as air.

Brian jutted out his chin. "Nobody's. I can't say."

"Ronnie Mayhew's?"

"No."

"Then whose?"

"Nobody's."

"Brian," cried Rachel, going to the boy, taking his sturdy face in her hands. "Talk to us, please. Tell us about it. We have to know."

He brushed her hands away. "There's nothing to tell, Mom. Nothing!"

David jumped forward and grabbed his son's arm. "Don't act like that with your mother," he said sternly. "Don't you dare act like that with her."

"It's no different than the way you treat her!"

"That's enough of your lip, boy!"

Brian relented. "I'm sorry," he muttered, shaking himself free.

"We just want to help you, Brian," Rachel said quietly. "Please let us help."

His eyes flashed fire. "I don't need help. Why are you two ganging up on me? I didn't do anything."

"We found pot in your room, Brian. That's something. That's plenty," David said caustically.

Rachel interrupted. "Can't we just sit down and talk about this calmly?"

David heaved a sigh. "All right. Let's sit down, Brian."

The boy took a retreating step backward. "What for?"

"So we can talk, you, your mother and I."

Brian's eyes darted from parent to parent. "There's nothing to talk about."

David stepped forward and seized his son's collar. "I want to know if you're taking drugs!"

Brian choked out the words. "What difference...does it make?"

David tightened his grip. "Are you kidding me? What's wrong with your head, boy?"

"David, please," Rachel pleaded. "Let him go. If we all get angry, we won't get anywhere."

David looked at Rachel. The hard knot of fury in his expression loosened and fell away. "I'm sorry," he said, releasing the boy. Without anger animating his face David looked tired and drained. There was a slackening of his jowls, a sagging weariness around the jaw that gave Rachel a fleeting impression of an old man. He sat down in his recliner and rubbed his hands over his temples. Rachel and Brian sat down on the sofa, Brian sitting forward, head down, elbows on his knees.

"We have to get this thing worked out," insisted David. "This is serious, Brian. Can't you see this is a serious matter?"

"It's no big deal," Brian mumbled.

"Suppose you let your mother and me decide that, okay?"

"I guess," he said grudgingly.

David steadied his voice. "Now, what's the story, Brian?"

"Nothing. I was just doing a guy a favor."

"What do you mean, a favor?"

"This guy thought his old lady—his mother—was catching on, getting suspicious, so he asked if I'd stash the pot at my place for a while."

"And you thought that was perfectly all right to do?" asked David skeptically.

"Why not? I didn't smoke the joints, Dad. I was just helping him out for a few days."

David rubbed the back of his neck, as if to relieve a throbbing pain. "Do you really expect me to believe that, Brian?"

Brian stuck out his lower lip. "Believe what you want."

David straightened and stared hard at the boy. "Listen, I don't want any smart talk from you, son."

"I'm just telling it like it is. If you don't believe me—"

"How can I believe you? I don't know what's got into you lately. I don't even know you anymore."

"And you think I know you?" Brian stood and smoothed his jeans. "Can I go now?"

"Go? Go where?"

"To my room."

"You'll go to your room when I'm through with you, not before," David snapped. "Sit back down."

Brian dropped back onto the sofa, his eyes defiant, his arms crossed on his chest.

"Brian," said Rachel tentatively, "would you just tell us who gave you the drugs?"

He stared straight ahead. "I can't, Mom."

"Why not?"

"I promised him I wouldn't."

"But whoever he is, he needs help, Brian. Surely you can see that."

Brian's mouth snapped rigid; he stared at the floor, silent. He sat forward, hunched, his arms locked around his knees, his manner imperturbably stoic, truculent. Finally he said, "I don't want to talk anymore, Mom. Please let me go to my room. I feel sick."

"You stay where you are until we settle this," David said in exasperation.

Brian clutched his throat. "But, Dad, I think I'm going to throw up."

"David, please," said Rachel.

"All right, all right," David conceded reluctantly.

"But listen to me, Brian. You're on restriction. You are not to go out of this house for a month. You go to school and church and come home, that's it. No friends, no social activities, nothing. Do you understand?"

"Yeah, I get it," Brian said under his breath.

"And, Brian, I'm going to call the pastor and find out if he'll see the three of us tomorrow after church," said David. "We need help, Brian. Our family needs help. All three of us."

Brian's expression remained sullen, unresponsive, his emotions locked behind a wall of barely suppressed hostility. He pulled himself to his feet and trudged across the room, but Rachel had the impression of a wobbly marionette whose arms and legs might at any moment spring crazily in all directions. No matter how calm Brian seemed on the outside, Rachel knew he was flying apart inside, too stubborn to admit he needed help.

"Brian!" said David sharply, as if there surely must be more to say.

Brian stopped in his tracks and glared at his father. "Yeah, Dad?"

David seemed momentarily tongue-tied. "This—this isn't over, son. It's...just the beginning."

"Can I go to my room now, Dad?" Brian asked tonelessly.

David expelled a heavy sigh. "Yes, go on."

When Brian had gone down the hall and shut the door to his room, David looked across at Rachel and murmured, "I guess it's time for me to go, too."

Rachel nodded wordlessly, watching him. He stood and walked to the door, but stayed there, apparently reluctant to leave. He cracked his knuckles nervously.

Rachel went to him, facing him, unsure what to say. What could either of them say? They had just fought a small war with their son and had no idea who had won. Maybe in such wars there were no winners. "I'm sorry, Rae," he said softly.

She searched his eyes, saw the pain. "Sorry?"

"Sorrier than you'll ever know." He had a rumpled, weary look to him, his hair tousled like a little boy's, his eyes filled with a rare neediness. She had the feeling that, were she to encourage him, David might impulsively gather her into his arms. He might kiss her suddenly and tell her he wanted to stay. She almost welcomed his closeness, his touch. Almost. But that was not something for her to think about now.

"I'm sorry it went like this," he told her. "I had hoped we could clear this up. That Brian would be cooperative. I had hoped it was a false alarm."

"But you don't think it is?"

"I have no idea."

"What can we do now?" she asked.

"We'll talk with Pastor Emrick. Maybe he can reach Brian."

"Isn't there anything else we can do?" she urged, tears starting.

"Pray. I'm still new at that, but I believe prayer makes a difference."

She nodded. "I'm a little rusty, but I think God will understand."

"I'm going to contact Mr. Mayhew, Ronnie's father," said David, "to see if he knows anything about all of this. If he doesn't, he needs to be alerted."

"Then you do think Brian is protecting Ronnie Mayhew?"

"Who else?"

"You'll let me know if you find out anything?"

"Yes, I will."

She reached out instinctively and touched David's stubbled jaw. The solid warmth of his face sent a ripple of pleasure up her arm. "Good night, David."

"Good night, Rae." Before she realized what was happening, he reached out and drew her close and placed his palm lightly on the rounded swell of her abdomen. "At least this little one is safe and sound. Thank God for that."

"Yes," she murmured breathlessly, "thank God!"

David bent his face to hers and kissed her cheek. "I'll see you tomorrow, Rae, after church...with Brian. And don't forget our date next Friday night."

"I won't," she said with a wistful smile.

"I'm counting on that, Rae." He seemed to be staring into her very soul with eyes that were at once mesmerizing and disarming. "Until tomorrow, sweetheart."

"Yes. Tomorrow," she managed, feeling suddenly light-headed, faint. As absurd as it seemed, she didn't want to let him go. Even more irrational was this sudden, unsettling desire to take his hand and lead him to their room, to cuddle with him in their bed and fall asleep in his arms, to wake with him beside her in the morning.

Her face grew uncomfortably warm. She quickly pushed the idea away. She had closed that door months ago. Locked it forever. It was too late for romantic interludes. Too much had happened. All that made up a marriage, her marriage—love and faith and trust—had been destroyed. She and David could never go back. They would do well just to maintain a companionable friendship for the sake of their children. That was as much as she dared hope for now.

Chapter Nineteen

Rachel felt a certain anticipation about this evening, a vague expectancy that she could not define or deny. It was a feeling that made her just a little breathless. This wasn't a real date, she kept reminding herself. Not in the traditional sense. Why then did she feel such an undercurrent of excitement? Glancing at David beside her in his classy sports car as they headed for the freeway, she said, for the sake of conversation, "It's a perfect evening, isn't it?"

He laughed lightly, his eyes on the road. "Yes, it is. Can you believe May is nearly here already?"

"No, it's caught me completely by surprise," said Rachel. In spite of her burgeoning size, she felt pretty in a burgundy two-piece dress with soft pleats and a scalloped neckline. David had told her more than once tonight how lovely she looked. She gazed over at him now. In his banded-collar shirt and navy blue double-breasted suit, he had never looked more handsome. "Where does the time go, David?"

"I don't know, Rae, but may I tell you again how beautiful you look tonight?"

She smiled, pleased. "You've already told me several times."

"And I'll tell you again. I wish time would stand still so I could just look at you."

"Thank you," said Rachel, actually blushing. "Am I allowed to know where we're going or is it a surprise?"

"You'll see." He shot her a quick, knowing glance, grinning boyishly, then turned his attention back to his driving. After a moment he asked, "Did you get everything arranged for Brian?"

"Yes, he's having dinner at Marlene's, then spending the rest of the night in his room doing homework."

"Alone?"

"He said he was too old for a sitter, so we compromised. Marlene promised to check in on him during the evening."

"I guess that should be okay. We've got to trust him sometime, right?"

Rachel nodded. "Pastor Emrick talked about the importance of building trust as a family."

"It's not easy, is it?" said David quietly.

Rachel knew he was talking about more now than Brian. It was true. They all had a long way to go to rebuild trust. And even then, it might never happen.

David's sports car propelled them onto the Long Beach Freeway, lurching them into the outside lane where they joined the slow-moving queues of early-evening traffic. The sky was bathed in pastel-shaded dusk-oranges and yellows, a melting sherbet mixture, with the sun a solid scooped ball of cinnamon hovering precariously close to the earth. It was lovely, this time of evening, this sudden final blush of color on the horizon before night surged over everything, blotting out the landscape in a single sweep, pervasive and complete.

"You never answered me," said Rachel. "I asked if tonight is a surprise."

"A surprise?" mused David, gently mocking. "Well, that depends. Are you in the mood for barbecued sweet and sour spareribs, wonton soup, pork chow mein and the lightest almond cookies in the whole Los Angeles area?"

"And miniature china teapots of clear, very hot tea?" she said brightly, catching his enthusiasm. "And hand-carved chopsticks we can't possibly eat with?"

"You bet."

"Sounds wonderful to me."

"Great. There's this little place not far from here. It doesn't look too impressive from the outside, but it's quiet and the atmosphere is pleasant. I thought you'd like that better than a place with crowds and dazzling lights and jangling music."

She folded her hands in her lap. She hadn't felt so relaxed in weeks. "It sounds perfect, David."

His voice was buoyant with anticipation. "And after a leisurely meal, I thought we'd drive into Los Angeles to the Music Center. I have tickets for a symphony concert at the Dorothy Chandler Pavilion. I know how much you like that highbrow stuff. How does that itinerary sound?"

"I'd like that, David. The Music Center is beautiful. We were there once before, and it was lovely."

"I remember you liked it." His eyes swept over

her. "It won't be too tiring for you, will it? I mean, Junior's not acting up or anything?"

"No, Junior's doing just fine. Sometimes it bothers me to sit for long at a time, but if the baby acts up, maybe we could leave during an intermission."

"Sure, you just let me know. Just say the word."

She laughed. "Don't look so worried, David. I really don't expect any problems."

He uttered a sigh of relief. "Good. Just let me know. We don't want to take any chances with that little guy."

"Or girl," said Rachel with a smile.

"Yeah. Or girl," David said, grinning. "I tell you, Rachel, it's hard for me to imagine being a father again. It blows my mind. But I'm really stoked. Think of it, another little kid calling me Daddy."

"You really are excited about the baby?"

"Since the day I felt him doing a tap dance in your tummy, the kid's been real to me. I just hope I have the chance to be the kind of father he or she deserves." David's expression changed slightly, and he asked, "Tell me, how has Brian been this past week?"

Rachel thought a moment, her spirits ebbing slightly. "He's been very quiet. Keeps to himself. Hardly talks to me."

"Didn't Pastor Emrick's talk on Sunday have any effect on him?"

"I don't know. In a way, Brian seems obedient. He comes right home from school and does his homework. He's very polite. As far as I know he hasn't seen any of his friends, not even Ronnie, except perhaps at school."

"Good. That's a start. I just hope it's not too late,

Rachel. The talk you and I had with Pastor Emrick was a real eye-opener for me."

"What do you mean?"

"Well, he made me realize some gritty realities. Even though our salvation in Christ is secure, we still have a daily fight on our hands. I have a feeling it would be awfully easy for me to think of God as being created for me rather than me being created for Him."

"That's a strange thing to say," said Rachel candidly.

"I find myself thinking that God can do this for me and He can do that and if only He would make this happen—you know, a job, things settled with Brian, our problems solved...."

"I do that, too, David. I get terribly perturbed or impatient if God doesn't work something out the way I think it should be."

David nodded but kept his eyes on the road.

"It boils down to me at the center of things, with God at the periphery, and that's not right. Pastor Emrick knocked me over when he said, 'When our lives are truly God-centered, *Christ-centered*, then all the other things fall into place.' Like, how do you do that?"

Rachel made a pleased, chuckling sound low in her throat.

David glanced over at her. "Are you laughing at me?"

"Not at all," she assured him. "I just can't believe this is you talking about spiritual things. It's so incredible. You're like this eager little baby Christian, trying to get all the answers and put all the pieces together."

He nodded, smiling. "I guess that's just what I am. To tell you the truth, it's like I traded in the old me for this new person that I don't quite know yet. I guess this born-again thing will always be a mystery to me. Pastor Emrick talked about obeying God. But how do we really obey God? Do you ever think about that, Rae?"

"Yes, a lot this week since our talk with the pastor. I've been reading my Bible and praying again. It feels good to be back in touch with the Lord."

"That's great, Rachel. Then you haven't let Brian's problem get you down?"

"Sometimes a wave of panic will go through me, but this peace I have goes deeper."

For a moment David was silent. While he lightly thumped his fingers on the steering wheel, his expression grew cloudy, curiously opaque. There was almost a haggard quality to the set of his jaw.

"Is anything wrong?" Rachel ventured.

"Not really," David replied. "It's just, after talking with Pastor Emrick, I realize I really blew it that night with Brian. I lost my cool and exploded, and Brian naturally retaliated. It works on me—the fact that I failed. It's going to take a lot of wisdom to deal with Brian, and I don't know if I can handle it."

"We have a long way to go with him," Rachel conceded.

"And it's not just Brian's problem, either. It's all three of us. I hope a few more sessions with Pastor Emrick will help. You and I have things to settle between us, Rachel, and we have things to settle with Brian."

"I know. It hurts to think Brian may be turning to

drugs because he's lacking something from his home life, something we should have been giving him."

"Yes, it is hard to accept," David agreed. "When Pastor Emrick suggested we needed treatment along with Brian, my first impulse was to punch him in the nose. Stupid, huh? I mean, this feeling just broke inside me, this overwhelming frustration. It tore me up inside to think I had failed at something as important as raising my own son."

Rachel nodded. "It's hard to approach this problem with Brian without feeling guilty and defeated."

"Don't worry, we'll make it, Rae," said David, hitting the turn signal for the next freeway off-ramp. They wound off onto a surface road and made a left turn. There was no longer any hint of color in the sky overhead, but the inky darkness was broken into pieces at the horizon by innumerable distant city lights—street lamps, freeway beacons, flashing neon signs, window lights gleaming from great, jutting high-rise buildings, and the strung-out glitter of shopping centers.

"By the way, did you contact Ronnie Mayhew's father?" asked Rachel, thinking still of Brian.

"Yes. I went to see him at his work. He has quite an impressive office—lots of marble and mahogany, plush carpets, ornate paintings. He's a vice president or general manager or something, I can't remember now."

"You didn't accuse Ronnie of anything, did you?"

"No, of course not. I just told Mr. Mayhew about the situation with Brian and suggested the possibility that Ronnie could be involved."

"What did he say?"

David gave his steering wheel a rhythmic tap. "He

blew up at me, nearly threw me out of his office. He said just because I was having problems with my boy, I had no right trying to get his son in trouble."

"Did he really say that?"

"He said his son has everything a boy could want and has no reason to fool around with drugs."

"Then you didn't get anywhere with him?"

"Nowhere."

"I'm sorry, David. I felt sure Ronnie was involved."

"I'm sure he is."

A thoughtful silence fell between the two of them until, in a little Los Angeles suburb that Rachel didn't recognize, David swung his sports car into a narrow driveway separating a brick building from a busy taco stand with signs advertising two tacos for the price of one and free balloons for the kiddies. Rachel watched as customers worked their way through ragged lines toward a window to receive cardboard boxes of food in orange wrappers. Children, milling about, tore off the wrappers and devoured tacos and enchiladas. There was a carnival hysteria about the place that both attracted and repelled Rachel.

She watched until David brought his car to a stop behind the brick building. This place stood in sharp contrast to the circus atmosphere nearby. Having few windows and a narrow, garishly painted door, the structure seemed impervious to the world, a blockade, a bastion, cryptic and hushed as a tomb.

David smiled faintly and said, "It doesn't look like much from the outside, but, believe me, the food is great."

"I think it looks...extraordinary," said Rachel, laughing, feeling within herself a sudden, rising pleasure from the presence of this man, her husband...a stranger who was finally becoming her friend.

Chapter Twenty

It was nearly eleven o'clock when Rachel and David left the Dorothy Chandler Pavilion. They took their time walking to the car, entranced, the music still swirling in their heads. The air smelled especially clean tonight, with the wafting fragrance of roses and bougainvillea touching them with magic, invigorating them. When they reached David's automobile, he helped Rachel into the passenger seat and asked, "Are you tired, honey?"

"Not very," she said, smiling.

As he settled into the driver's seat and started the engine, he said, "I want to talk to you about something, Rae. Would you like to take a drive along the ocean?"

She hesitated for only a moment. "All right. But shouldn't we call Brian first?"

"It's late. He'll be asleep by now. Do you feel tired?"

"No, I'm fine, really."

His gaze moved over her approvingly. "Did you enjoy the concert?"

"Yes, it was wonderful. And the dinner was perfect, too. I don't know when I've had such a nice evening, David."

"I'm glad you had a good time. I did, too. Sort of like old times."

"Yes," she murmured wistfully.

They took the Harbor Freeway out of Los Angeles and later drove down Ocean Boulevard to Belmont Shore, where they found a narrow stretch of beach accessible from the road. David pulled over to the side and turned off the ignition.

"How's this?" he said, shifting in his seat to face Rachel.

She gazed around. "I love the view…what I can see of it."

"But? I hear a distinct reservation in your voice."

"But it seems kind of strange being here. I mean, parking like this at the beach, like teenagers or something."

David moved his arm around the back of the seat, not quite touching her shoulder. "I could have taken you home, Rae, but Brian would be there. I wanted our talk to be private. Just us."

"All right, David." She was acutely aware of his closeness, his hand nearly brushing her back. She chided herself. Her heart was already pounding like a lovesick girl's.

"Hey, what did you do with those little fortune cookies?" he asked. "Where are they?"

Rachel laughed, a little embarrassed. "They're in my purse." She opened her handbag, pulled out a napkin and spread it open on what was left of her lap.

"You're laughing at me," she said, amiably accusing him. "You think I'm silly to save these, but I'll bet you're hungry now, aren't you?"

"All right, I'm game. Give me a fortune cookie."

"See, I told you. Wait, David, you have to read what it says—the little paper inside. Don't eat the paper."

Chuckling, David broke open the cookie, removed the narrow strip of paper and held it up to the window where enough street light penetrated the glass to bring the words into focus. "'Do something nice for someone near.'"

"What?"

"You heard me—my fortune, compliments of Hong Kong."

"Here's mine. Can you read it?"

He held the narrow slip up to the light and read, "'You will make friends with a stranger.'"

"A stranger? Wonderful. Who?"

"Me. How about me?"

She laughed lightly. "You're not a stranger, David."

"But I am," he said solemnly. His eyes glinted in the darkness, filled with a disturbing intensity. "We're all strangers, Rachel. That's what we've been, a family of strangers."

"Now you're getting serious," she warned softly. "These cookies are a joke, David, something to laugh at. They don't mean anything."

"I'm not talking about fortune cookies, Rachel. I'm talking about us, you and me. We have to talk and face things and make some decisions."

"I know, David, but—"

"Rachel, listen to me, listen."

She clasped her hands in her lap, fingering the fortune cookie. "I am listening, David."

"There's something I need to tell you."

"Not bad news, I hope."

"No. Good news. At least, I hope you'll think it's good. I've been offered a job with an engineering firm in Cleveland."

"Cleveland?"

"I know it's far away, but I can't keep collecting unemployment week after week. And there aren't that many jobs available here right now."

"But why Cleveland?"

David's voice rose, urgent, agitated. "I've had my application in all over the place, Rae, you know that, including a few places back East. This is the only promising thing to turn up. I've looked into the offer. It's a fantastic opportunity. A promotion, really. A management position. And the benefits package alone is incredible. I really feel I should take it."

Rachel stared at her hands. They felt tight, stiff. "When will you leave?"

His voice took on a persuasive lilt. "I was hoping you'd say you'll go with me. My parents don't live far from Cleveland. A half-hour drive at most. It would be good for Brian to be around his grandparents, not to mention giving him a whole new change of scene. A fresh start. You must know he needs that. You—"

Rachel raised her hand in protest. "Wait a minute, David. You're going too fast. Are you saying you want us to move to Ohio? All of us? Now? Just like that?"

"Not tomorrow or the next day, but soon, yes. If I

accept, they'll give me until June so Brian can finish out the school term."

Rachel began to tremble. Perhaps it was the night air or the shock of David's announcement, or her own rising indignation and incredulity. "I can't believe you'd do this to me, David."

"What are you talking about? Do what?"

"Make me believe this was just a pleasant evening out, when you really planned to hit me with this news. How can you ask me to consider something so big when our lives are such a mess?"

An edge of defensiveness crept into David's voice. "I thought I was sharing good news. I thought you'd be pleased."

"How can I be pleased? A move like this—it's the last straw to tear our family apart."

"How can you say that? I want you to go with me. You and Brian and the baby. I want us to be a family again."

"I can't, David," she said shakily. "I can't just pick up the pieces of our marriage and go with you to Ohio."

"Please, Rae, don't say no." He ran his fingertips lightly over her shoulder. "Will you at least think about it? Pray about it?"

Rachel put her face in her hands. "Oh, David, you've got me so confused, I don't know what to say."

"All right, Rachel. I won't push you." David was still holding pieces of the fortune cookie. He lifted them ceremoniously in the palm of his hand. "Here's to our silly fortune cookies, Rae. It says, 'Do something nice for someone near.' I can do that." He leaned over and kissed her full on the lips. She did not move; she hardly breathed. Only her fingers moved as she mindlessly wound her own fortune cookie into her napkin, twisting the edges of the flimsy paper into white ragged snakes.

David removed the napkin from her hands and let it fall to the floor of the vehicle, swallowed by darkness. Gently he took Rachel in his arms, holding her with an exquisite tenderness, and kissed her again, touching his lips to her forehead and eyes, to her lashes, moving his mouth over her ear to the softness of her hair. His kisses had never tasted so sweet, but the lingering ache in her heart made them bittersweet. "David, no," she whispered. He held her head against his shoulder and caressed the back of her neck until at last she pulled away from him.

"David, don't," she said again.

"Rachel, please."

"David, I'm uncomfortable," she protested. "I have to sit back."

He released her. "Darling, are you all right?"

"Yes, but I'm very tired. I can't—"

"Rachel, listen to me." He turned her face to his. "You're my wife. I want you to be my wife. In a few weeks you're going to have my child. That baby needs us together. Brian needs us together. What do I have to say to get through to you?"

Rachel was silent. A war raged inside her—the desire to surrender to the man she loved and the impulse to flee the prospect of being hurt again. Her chin puckered as tears gathered behind her eyes.

David drew her to him again and sought her lips. This time Rachel recognized within herself a wish to respond. But the desire was unsettled, fleeting and evanescent as air, like the moist sea air seeping into the automobile. She wanted to let herself feel intensely, yearned to be sure of her feelings, to wash away the sediment of bitterness and erase the scars. How did one erase scars? *Oh, God, what can I do?*

Then she became aware of something. A sound. This man—her husband—who sat close beside her, his breathing strained, his breath pungent but sweet, relinquished his embrace and put his hands over his face and wept. His voice was muffled, breaking over waves of deep, sweeping emotion. "I'm sorry, Rachel. I don't know what else to do. I love you, but I can't reach you. Should I leave you alone? Go away? What?"

Stunned, shaken, she murmured, "I—I don't know. I want to love you again, David, I do, but..."

"Rae, if it's the Ohio job, I'll turn it down. I'll tell them I can't take it."

She gazed at him in astonishment. "You'd do that for me? Give up what could be the opportunity of a lifetime?"

Tears glinted in David's eyes. "Whatever it takes, darling, to prove you come first in my life. I love you."

She searched his eyes. "Do you really, David?"

He traced the curve of her lips. "More than I ever dreamed it was possible to love a woman." His voice softened, became almost a whisper. "Loving God makes me love you all the more."

"I want to love you, David." Rachel's voice was full of yearning. "But there's been so much hurt between us. How can I open myself to more hurt?"

"What can I say, except...I'm sorry. I was wrong. Will you forgive me for hurting you?"

A tear escaped. "All I ever wanted was to know you loved me."

"I do. I love you. You know I do."

"Yes, I'm beginning to believe..."

"Then love me back, Rachel, please..."

"Help me, David...."

Again he swept her into his arms and kissed her slowly, with an astounding tenderness born out of anguish and longing. "Please forgive me, Rachel," he whispered against her lips. "Love me, darling."

And Rachel, loosing the reins on her heart, at last broke through the bonds of bitterness that shackled her emotions. Slowly, inevitably, she surrendered to that familiar swell of joy, of love, of acceptance and forgiveness. With delicious abandon, she returned her husband's kiss.

When David released her, he was breathless, gleeful. "Darling, I'm so happy I could—" he searched for words "—I could run on the beach...shout our love to the stars."

She was breathless, too, giddy with delight. "Why not paint our love across the sky in brilliant letters?" she teased.

He took her hand. "All right. Come on. Run with me in the sand. What do you say?"

She laughed and pulled away. "You're crazy, out of your mind, David. I'm as big as an elephant."

He reached for the door handle. "I'll help you. I won't let you fall."

She stifled her laughter. "No, David, don't be silly. Walk on the beach this time of year? Never!"

"You're right. Forget the beach." He clasped her hand to his mouth and gently kissed her fingers.

"Who needs the beach? We have each other. We can go home, Rae. Home where we belong."

"Home?" she echoed, reading his meaning. "Yes, home."

"You understand, Rachel," he said softly. "Tonight we go home together. To our own room. Our own bed."

She pressed his hand against her cheek, delighting in its warmth. "Yes, that's good," she whispered. "I want you home. In every way."

It was well past midnight when David unlocked the door for Rachel and flicked the light switch in the hallway. Arm in arm, they ambled in together with a certain conspiratorial air, a sweet sense of abandonment, as if they were incredibly young lovers meeting for a romantic tryst.

Helping her off with her coat, he gently kissed the back of her neck, his lips moving tantalizingly to her shoulder and around to the hollow of her throat. Happily, dreamily, she kicked off her shoes and flung her purse on a chair as he drew her to him for a caress. As he held her in a close embrace, she could feel the baby wriggle and kick between them, protesting. They both laughed.

David's hand caressed her bounteous abdomen. "Tell Junior to settle down," he murmured. "Tell him it's just his mommy and daddy stealing a kiss."

"I think he's getting a little tired of his crowded quarters," said Rachel with a sigh.

David smiled. "He's got a point. Not much room in there to play soccer or throw a curve ball."

She leaned heavily against David. "He's not the only one who's tired."

He supported her with his arms. "Let me get you to bed, Rae."

"But shouldn't we wake Brian and tell him you're home?"

"No, let's tell him in the morning." David kissed the soft curls brushing her cheek. "Besides, he'll know when he sees me here."

"He'll be so excited—"

The telephone rang, startling them, jangling their nerves, shattering their splendid mood. Rachel stared at the phone as if waking from a dream. "Who...it's so late...who could be—"

"Probably a wrong number. I'll get it," said David.

"Hurry! Before it wakes Brian!"

David grappled with the phone and barked huskily into the receiver. "Hello? Yes?"

Watching, waiting, Rachel shifted her weight from one stockinged foot to the other, then sank onto the sofa and absently patted her hair into place, listening.

"Yes, Mrs. Webber's here," said David, sounding puzzled. "Who's calling, please? What? Well, this is Mr. Webber, Brian's father. I'm sorry, I don't understand. There must be some mistake. No, my son is here, asleep in his room. Just a moment." He turned to Rachel, motioning something.

"Brian? Is it about Brian?" she asked.

"Check his room," David whispered, a clipped, unmistakable urgency in his tone. He spoke into the phone again. "We're checking right now."

Rachel heaved herself up and moved as swiftly as she could, but her steps were sluggish, as if she were swaying in slow motion, getting nowhere, struggling against dark waves of an imaginary sea. Her return from Brian's room was worse, a nightmare. "He's not there, David," she cried shrilly. "He's not in his room. He's gone!"

David went deathly white, his jaw tightening, his eyes flashing with a fierce intensity. He put his mouth to the receiver and said brokenly, "It's our son. We'll be right over. Do whatever's necessary. We're on our way."

Rachel stared at her husband without comprehension. "What is it? What happened?"

A grisly, spangled vision illumined David's eyes as he uttered, "That was the hospital. It's Brian. He was in a car accident tonight."

Chapter Twenty-One

The drive to the hospital was insufferably long, a ghastly trip interrupted by hideous traffic lights that brought David's sports car to a stop again and again. An irony, so many stop lights, when all along the streets were empty of traffic. So why the demanding lights, forcing David to wait long precious moments for nothing in the empty streets?

Rachel twisted her handkerchief and stared through the windshield, barely aware of the muted car sounds grinding a million miles away. One encompassing fear gripped her: *Brian, Brian, Brian. What about Brian?*

Brian had been in a car crash. She didn't even know if he was dead or alive!

She ground her polished fingernails into her palm. Was she trembling? She was numb, suspended somehow, her senses revolving around that one focal point. Brian.

They were approaching the hospital now. Rachel stared ahead, stunned by the reality of buildings and grounds, sturdy, blank structures that held a secret. She would have to pry that secret out of those silent walls; the secret was Brian. Brian—a mystery, a puzzle, an unknown factor.

The hospital was an ordinary building—familiar, really. Made of stucco, a buff color. Old. Spanish architecture or something similar, with a sort of cloistered patio area at the entrance. It stood on a slight hill. The street in front of the hospital was narrow, making it difficult to pass cars or to circumvent automobiles parked at the curb. Brian had been born in this hospital, so certainly it was familiar, a dusty, forgotten familiarity.

Now Brian was here again.

Only not in the maternity wing where Rachel had been to tea just two weeks ago. It was one of those teas for prospective mothers, providing them with an opportunity to preregister so that they could check in to the hospital later without the usual red tape. Rachel remembered that afternoon. A convivial coffee klatch, during which a score of chattering, excited, very pregnant women were given a token tour of the maternity ward and alternative birth center, then subjected to a flowery speech by some middle-aged woman, who may or may not have had children, on the joys of motherhood. Rachel had spent this time making out a shopping list.

Rachel's thoughts were sliced in two by the rumbling of David's car as he pulled into the parking lot. The parking lot was an interminable distance from the hospital itself. Rachel's head ached with a pounding that was like words, beating over and over, saying something. It seemed to Rachel that she was on the verge of realizing some vital truth, something about

Brian that would make him real to her, no longer a mystery. But the idea remained fuzzy in her mind and never actually assumed a particular shape. In fact, nothing was in focus. Everything blurred as if shot through with rain.

Although the headache remained, Rachel's mind turned blank as they strode toward the hospital entrance. Her body seemed empty. Yet it was heavy and dragged her down, and the child within her twisted and turned periodically, reminding her of his presence. This movement within her was more real than the actual outward movements involved in climbing out of the car and dashing breathlessly toward the hospital door.

This was like a dream, composed of scattered fragments of reality. Brian was supposed to have had dinner with Marlene. He had promised to spend the night studying in his room. He should have been home sound asleep in his own bed. Instead, he was in this hospital and she didn't even know if he was alive or dead.

How could this be real? Only one thing was real: the mystery of Brian. What terrible accident had happened that strangers should call for her in the middle of the night? What hideous sequence of events had led up to the horror of this moment? An accident. Brian in an accident.

What about Brian? What was he doing when she saw him last? What was he wearing? Tennis shoes, his blue striped shirt? No, the brown one—the blue one was missing a button. He had said, "I need this shirt fixed for school on Monday. The button's gone." He was reading a book at the time, history or geography or something, something about Mesopotamia. The dawn of civilization. He had promised her that after having dinner at Marlene's he would spend the evening studying, writing a report. He would be fine. She should have a good time; say hello to Dad.

There was a great gap between that moment of pleasant, ordinary conversation and this present moment of frenzy, of horror. What had happened between? Dear God, what?

Her guilt was back. *My son may be dying while I was out on a date. Oh, God, dear God!*

Inside the hospital the atmosphere was hushed, a strict, ritualistic observance of silence. The foyer was nearly empty. The corridor seemed empty except for an occasional phantom shadow of a nurse or an orderly slipping in or out of a room. Even these few actions, performed anonymously by people in anonymous white outfits, seemed accomplished without sounds, no footsteps, no rustling of clothing, no hum of conversation. Rachel's own breathing was louder and more demanding than the accumulated sounds of this building.

They were in the foyer. David gripped her arm, holding tightly, trying to steer her somewhere. The foyer, with muted overhead lights, was pleasantly dim. Partitions and offices were to the left. Beside the information desk, artificial plants stood in plastic containers that looked like something more expensive—wood or stone, not plastic. The plants were too green and shiny, mere imitations.

Rachel stared toward the information desk. Someone was there, a white-haired woman with a bland face, thinly penciled brows and tidy, precise lips. She was writing something down, filling in blank spaces, very neat and exact.

David went straight to the desk, gave his name and started bombarding her with questions. Where was Brian? How was he? What had happened?

The woman smiled kindly and handed David some official forms. "These should be signed before any underage person is admitted to the hospital. If you would take care of that now—"

"Forget your paperwork," David exploded. "My son—where is he?"

The woman's answers were as neat and exact as her handwriting. Brian was in the emergency room. Dr. Whalen, the emergency room physician, was in attendance. Everything was being done. No, there were no details. Rachel and David should go to the ER waiting room and wait for someone to come and talk to them, to explain. She would call ahead and let Emergency know they were coming.

Reluctantly, David and Rachel made their way to the ER waiting room and sat down on one of the sleek green vinyl couches. Wire magazine racks and polished tables were mixed in among the bright, shiny couches and chairs. Rachel stared at the walls and the corridors shooting off to nowhere. The walls seemed transparent and tediously repetitious. It was as if Rachel could see all the rooms and halls, an incredible labyrinth. She could imagine the complex maze composed of endless cubicles housing flesh-and-blood bodies, all sick or impaired, all needing attention.

Rachel could smell the sickness, although it was masked by other smells of products used to clean away the odors of the flesh, of weakness and of death. Chlorine, disinfectants, soaps. Rachel could smell them all. They absorbed the air and changed it.

This place was not like the rest of the world. It was

not natural. Too much was covered up. Illness was a business here, tidy, orderly, a matter of computerized cards and signatures on dotted lines.

What was she doing here? Waiting for Brian? It was a lie. Brian wasn't here. There was nothing here of Brian.

"What are you thinking about?" David's voice. Sounding concerned.

She licked her dry lips. "What? What did you say?"

"Your expression—what are you thinking?" asked David.

"Nothing. Brian. Where is he? What's happening?"

"I don't know."

"They should let us go to him. How can they keep us away? How? Why?"

David shook his head wearily. "We just have to wait."

She clutched his arm, her nails sinking into the nubby fabric of his jacket. "We must do something, David. We can't just sit here."

"Do you want me to call the pastor?"

"Pastor Emrick? No. What can he do? It's the middle of the night. I want the doctor."

"I just thought—"

"No, let Pastor Emrick sleep. Wait till we find out something. Maybe Brian's all right. Maybe we can take him home."

"I pray to God—!"

Suddenly there was a sound, the banging of a door. A stylishly dressed woman and a man in a business suit entered the ER waiting room, plainly agitated and in a hurry. The man was boisterous; his every movement seemed exaggerated. He went straight to the information desk, demanding something, wanting to know what was going on. The admitting clerk hushed him with waves of her hand and leaned forward gingerly to speak, to offer information perhaps. The man listened, squint-eyed, his mouth poised for quick rebuttal or contradiction. He did not want to listen. He had things to say. He began to argue, pacing about like a man who had demands to make.

The woman with him stepped back a little, giving him room. She was slender, attractive, a pleasant contrast to the man. She wore a rust-colored pantsuit, slightly tailored, sophisticated, with a crisp, flared jacket. After a moment she went to the man, gently touching his arm, saying something. He waved her off, still talking to the woman behind the ER check-in desk. The clerk answered him with low, clipped phrases, then looked away, at her papers, apparently dismissing him.

"I know him," said David, leaning forward attentively.

"What?"

"That man. He's Ronnie Mayhew's father."

"What's he doing here?"

"I'll find out." David got up and crossed the room to Mr. Mayhew and spoke quietly, soberly, to both the man and the woman. After a moment he brought them back to Rachel.

"This is my wife, Rachel," he said as Rachel stood and extended her hand. "Rachel, Darryl Mayhew. And Mrs. Mayhew."

"Karen," said the woman politely.

"I understand they've got your boy here, too," boomed Darryl Mayhew, red faced.

"Yes," said Rachel faintly. "That's what they said."

"Ronnie's here, but I can't find out a thing. Those doggone nurses are as closemouthed as corpses."

"Do you know anything about the accident—what happened, how they are?" asked Rachel anxiously.

"How would I know what happened? Probably some sort of fender bender. You know how it is. Doctors gotta get permission just to treat a hangnail."

"I pray that's all it is," said Rachel.

"Was your boy driving?" asked Mayhew.

"No, he's only thirteen."

Mayhew raked his fingers through his thinning hair. "We raced over here from north Hollywood, left an important social engagement right in the middle of things. I'll have to pay for that, I tell you. Money, contracts—it's costing me. But I'm here now and I want answers."

"We're waiting, too," said David.

"We got a call from the police," said Karen Mayhew. "Our housekeeper must have given them Darryl's pager number. They said there was an accident, but they wouldn't give us any details. Just that several young people were brought in, including Ronnie. We have no idea how bad it was. We don't even know where it happened or who was driving."

"If it was Ronnie, I'll ground that boy for the rest of his life," said Mayhew. "I've told him a million times to watch his driving. But when these kids first get their license they think they're invincible."

"Brian was supposed to be home studying," said Rachel distractedly. "He promised. He wasn't even supposed to be out."

"Kids today don't mind," said Mayhew. "They've

got their own agenda. They do as they please and don't care who they hurt, including themselves."

Karen turned to Rachel. "Darryl signed a treatment form or something. What did she call it, Darryl? Did they ask you to sign one, too?"

Rachel nodded. "And then the nurse told us we have to wait for the doctor. And who knows how long that could be?"

Darryl Mayhew paced the floor. "Well, if these high and mighty doctors think I'm going to wait around all night without answers, they've got another thing coming. They'd better get their tails out here pronto, or I tell you, I'll..."

While Mayhew stormed, Rachel's attention turned to something else. Down the corridor came two uniformed policemen walking with a purposeful stride, their robust frames ramrod straight, their eyes shadowed with a grim intensity. Something in their solemn expressions sent off a warning signal in Rachel's brain. Even before the men spoke, she knew they were coming with crucial answers...or urgent questions...or both.

Chapter Twenty-Two

The two policemen introduced themselves as Sergeant Bruner and Sergeant Hindman. "Mr. and Mrs. Webber, Mr. and Mrs. Mayhew, we're investigating the accident your sons were involved in earlier tonight," said Sergeant Bruner, a swarthy man with a wrestler's muscled torso. "We'd like to ask you a few questions."

"We don't know anything," said Darryl Mayhew fiercely. "We've been trying to get answers for over an hour."

"Maybe we can help each other, Mr. Mayhew," said Sergeant Hindman, taller and leaner than Bruner. "We'll give you some answers and you give us some."

"The accident—what happened?" cried Rachel. "Were you there?"

"Yes. My partner and I were dispatched to the scene. We arrived just before the ambulance," said Bruner.

"It happened on the corner of Long Beach Boulevard and Pacific Coast Highway,'' said Hindman. ''A silver '95 Mustang ran a red light and broadsided a small pickup.''

''Ronnie's car,'' said Darryl Mayhew, blanching.

''Yes, sir. Neither boy was wearing a seat belt.''

Rachel clasped her hand over her mouth. She was going to be sick. ''Is Brian...alive?''

''Yes, ma'am, but you'll have to talk to the doctor about his condition. And the other boy's, too.''

David slipped his arm around Rachel and held her close. ''You'd better sit down, Rae. Come on.''

''No, not until I know everything. What else can you tell us, Sergeant Hindman?''

His mouth tightened. He cast a glance at his partner and drew in a sharp breath. ''Does your son take drugs, Mr. Webber?''

''No,'' said Rachel.

''Are you sure?''

She wasn't.

''Does he drink?''

''No...I don't think so.''

''Well, we found beer and marijuana in the Mustang. We won't be sure until we get the toxicology reports and blood tests from the hospital, but it looked like both boys were under the influence.''

''Oh, dear God, no!'' she prayed aloud. Rachel swayed against David. Everything reeled for a terrifying moment. Her head was spinning; she was going down.

But David caught her in his strong arms and held her close. ''Rachel, you really must sit down.''

''No, not yet. I've got to find out about Brian.''

Sergeant Bruner cleared his throat uneasily. ''Mr.

Webber, Mr. Mayhew, did you have any idea your sons had drugs and alcohol in their possession?''

''No,'' said Darryl Mayhew indignantly. ''It must have been the Webber boy. Ronnie knows better than to mess with drugs.''

''What about it, Mr. Webber? You know anything about your son experimenting with drugs?''

A tendon tightened along David's jaw. Reluctantly he said, ''Not long ago Rachel discovered some marijuana cigarettes in Brian's room. He claimed they belonged to a friend. He didn't say who. Since then Brian's been on restriction.''

''Until tonight, you mean.''

''He was supposed to be at home studying,'' said Rachel. ''Our neighbor was keeping an eye on him.''

''I see,'' said Bruner. ''But it looks more like those boys had partying in mind.''

Karen Mayhew turned to her husband. ''Darryl, do you suppose Ronnie raided your liquor cabinet?''

''Shut up, Karen,'' Mayhew growled under his breath.

''That's a lethal combination, you know,'' warned Sergeant Hindman. ''Alcohol and drugs, that's bad, real bad.''

''What do you know about my son, Sergeant? You must know something,'' said Karen Mayhew earnestly. ''Please tell me. Will Ronnie be all right?''

''You'll have to wait for the doctor, Mrs. Mayhew.''

''And you do understand that we'll have to question both boys as soon as they're able to talk,'' said Sergeant Bruner. ''We'll be going now, but we'll be back in touch...soon.''

"We hope the boys will make a full recovery," said Sergeant Hindman with a solemn nod.

"Wait," said David. "What about the other car? Was anyone hurt?"

"The driver, but not seriously," said Bruner. "The Mustang hit the truck bed. A few seconds earlier it would have hit the cab and maybe killed the driver."

"My boy's in bad trouble, isn't he?" snapped Darryl Mayhew. "I suppose the man will sue. Everybody sues these days. Ronnie will have to go to court. There'll be a scandal. Am I right? Just tell me. Am I right?"

"Perhaps for now you should just worry about getting your son out of the hospital and on his feet again," suggested Sergeant Hindman. "Good night, Mr. and Mrs. Mayhew, Mr. and Mrs. Webber."

"We're in for it now, Karen," warned Darryl Mayhew hotly when the policemen had gone. "I tell you, we're in for it. Those cops don't say anything. They can't tell you a thing. But I know we're in for it."

"What are we going to do, Darryl?" Karen asked feebly, her hands fluttering like white wounded birds.

"I'll tell you what I'm going to do. I'm going to kill that boy," he growled. "He can't do this to me. I've given him everything he could ask for, everything. Did I say no last month when he wanted his driver's license and his own car the day he turned sixteen? Did I ever once say no? And this is how he repays me!"

Karen Mayhew turned sadly to Rachel. "Ronnie is so independent, so set on doing his own thing. I try to talk to him, but he won't listen to reason. I try. What else can I do?"

Rachel nodded mechanically. She was in a daze.

She had heard too many words and nothing made sense. It was too much for her, too much to absorb. Her body and mind felt weighed down, heavy, like a great rock falling to the earth. David was right. She had to go sit down, quickly.

"Dear, you look so tired," said Karen Mayhew, following Rachel over to the couch. "Your baby is due soon, isn't it?"

"Yes, in a month. But it feels like it could be tonight."

The woman made a helpless gesture as if somehow to ease Rachel's discomfort. Then with a baffled shrug she joined Rachel on the couch. Next to this woman Rachel felt awkward and ugly and elephantine, a gross shapeless mass beside a lovely, fortyish sophisticate. Rachel's new dress was a rumpled mess. The baby pounded inside her, twisting, squirming. He was pulling her down, pressing her down, so that she might never get up again. And Brian. *Oh, God,* she silently prayed, *what of Brian?*

Then, as she stared down the hall, her gaze fleeting and unfocused, a lanky, dark-haired man in surgical greens came out of a room and stopped to speak a moment with a nurse. He looked grimly toward Rachel, surveying the four of them in a glance, appraising them, a curious, impersonal gaze. Finally he walked toward them, a sober, self-assured stride.

"Mr. and Mrs. Webber? Mr. and Mrs. Mayhew?"

"Yes," said David. "Doctor...?"

"Yes, I'm Dr. Whalen."

"It's about time," said Darryl Mayhew loudly. "I want to know about Ronnie."

"You're Mr. Mayhew?"

"Yes. How is my son?"

"He's been taken to his room in the medical wing, Mr. Mayhew. He's battered and bruised. Has a couple of cracked ribs and some ugly facial cuts. But so far so good. He was rambling a bit when they brought him in, his speech slurred, but he came around about an hour ago. He's going to be all right once the high wears off. Naturally, we'll keep him for seventy-two hours for observation."

"Thank God he's okay! Can we see him?" asked Karen Mayhew, rubbing her hands together nervously. "Please let us see him."

"Just for a moment. Check with the nurse at the desk." He paused, apparently drawing his words together carefully. With a deliberate attempt at casualness, he said, "Oh, and Mr. and Mrs. Mayhew, it's too late to do anything tonight perhaps, but I would suggest you contact your family physician sometime tomorrow. I suspect your son has a drug problem. A *serious* drug problem."

Glaring momentarily at the doctor, Darryl Mayhew pivoted and stalked off down the hall, muttering something, his eyes malicious slits in his puffy, reddened face. Karen Mayhew clattered softly after him in her neat, expensive black stacked heels. Shrugging her slight shoulders helplessly, she turned her head and mumbled something back at them. The words scattered and fell on the air, and no one understood her. Rachel smiled wanly and Dr. Whalen nodded politely and was still nodding when Rachel asked about Brian.

Dr. Whalen dragged a chair over to the couch and sat down. David sat beside Rachel, circling her shoulder with his arm. "How is Brian?" he asked anxiously, no longer masking his concern.

"Mr. Webber, our primary concern is a nasty head injury. We've also treated your son for multiple contusions and bruises. And we're checking for internal injuries."

"Dear God, no!" Rachel whispered. She was trembling suddenly with a chill that rippled through her like a seismic shock.

"A head injury?" repeated David. "What does that mean? A concussion? Brain damage? What?"

Dr. Whalen chose his words carefully. "Your son was lethargic and unresponsive when they brought him in. And there was some forceful vomiting—"

Rachel broke in, dry mouthed, stammering. "How—how bad is he?"

Dr. Whalen tented his fingertips. "There's swelling inside the skull, Mrs. Webber."

"Bleeding?"

"It could be. Any accumulation of blood could put pressure on the brain and cause damage—"

"How much damage?" she pressed.

"The next twenty-four to seventy-two hours should tell the story."

David frowned. "That long, Doctor?"

"What are you doing for my son?" Rachel shrilled.

Dr. Whalen's voice remained smooth as silk. "At this moment careful observation is our best tool. Skull X rays have ruled out bone fragments in the brain."

"And the bad news?" questioned David.

"It's too soon to think in terms of bad news."

"But I hear it in your voice," David challenged. "What aren't you telling us?"

"We're not sure whether we're dealing with a subdural hematoma or..." His voice trailed off. "That's our biggest concern, Mr. Webber. You see, your son has slipped into a coma."

"A coma?" cried Rachel. "Are you saying he might never wake up? He—he could die? Not my son!"

"We'll continue running tests and monitoring vital signs, Mrs. Webber. We just have to wait and see."

"When can we see him?" said David over a groundswell of emotion. "Where is Brian?"

Dr. Whalen hesitated. "Your son has been taken to the intensive care unit, Mr. Webber. In your wife's condition, perhaps..."

Rachel stared at him. "He's my son, Doctor. But why intensive care? Ronnie Mayhew's in the medical wing."

"The Mayhew boy was lucky. Your son needs help breathing."

"It's that bad?" said David, stunned. "Brian needs a machine to help him breathe?" An urgency sharpened David's voice. "I want to see my son—now!"

Dr. Whalen stood. "I'll take you to him."

Mutely David and Rachel followed the doctor down the hall to the intensive care unit. Words pounded inside Rachel's skull as she entered the room and approached Brian's bedside. *Coma. Respirator.* The words were going to explode inside her mind and scatter her senses all over the polished floor.

Instead, her mind went blank with horror as she saw Brian. He was bruised and swollen and deathly pale, smothered by a forbidding array of tubes, bandages and machinery. His bare, angular chest rose and fell with the gushing sound of the respirator. A shot of darkness cut off Rachel's vision, then her sight returned with a flash like lightning. She swayed; her body was folding up like spaghetti. She was going down, down.

"Are you all right, Mrs. Webber?" inquired Dr. Whalen.

Rachel shook her head, clearing it. "Yes. But Brian. He looks so broken, so helpless."

Taking her son's motionless hand in hers, Rachel bent over the guardrails and kissed Brian's bruised cheek. "Mama's here, Brian. And Daddy too. We love you, darling."

Supporting Rachel with one arm, David leaned over the bed and gently massaged Brian's shoulder. "Hey, big guy, we're here for you," he said, his voice husky, emotion filled. "You get well, okay, son? We've got a lot of catching up to do, you and I."

Rachel looked over at the doctor. "When will Brian start breathing on his own again?"

Dr. Whalen cleared his throat, a deliberate, calculated cough as he steered them away from the bedside. "Very soon, we hope. The sooner the better. We're doing everything possible." He shifted his gaze—a certain restless gesture, as if this conversation were something he would like to dismiss. He walked with them back to the lobby, then turned to David and said, "On the forms you signed, you listed Dr. Richard Quinn as your family physician. He has been contacted and should be here shortly. There really isn't much else I can tell you now."

"But Brian will be all right? He will start breathing on his own again, won't he?" insisted Rachel, a terrible panic writhing up through her chest, suffocating her. "He will come out of the coma!"

The doctor offered a tentative smile. "We'll do everything we can, Mrs. Webber."

What else did the doctor say? His words were like thick, jumbled soup. Rachel was drowning in his words; she couldn't breathe. His words were fragments, knocking her down.

Rachel could not recall the doctor leaving. He had told her to go home and get some sleep. When she refused, he told David to go get some strong black coffee. It would be good for them, he said. David was getting the coffee. And the doctor went off somewhere, perhaps back to take care of Brian. Rachel didn't see him go.

The coffee was too hot and scorched Rachel's throat. Her throat burned. It felt raw. She kept drinking, drinking the coffee down, holding the foam cup to her lips until the black liquid was gone. It burned down through her chest into her stomach. At least it was making her feel something.

She and David sat together for hours. It seemed like hours. It wasn't really. Or perhaps it was. She would not go home. Perhaps someone would come with news. Perhaps Brian would wake and call for her, wanting her that instant. She would wait. She drank more coffee and made frequent trips down the hall to the ladies' room, where she inspected her pale face in the mirror beneath the fluorescent lights. She was a ghost, with a vivid white sheen on her face and eerie shadows under her eyes. Her eyes were wide, unblinking, frightened bird's eyes.

The contractions that were a familiar part of Rachel's days lately were increasing noticeably tonight. The gradual tightening across her hardened abdomen was no longer merely a passing discomfort; it was becoming pain, demanding her attention. Rachel told herself this happened when she was tired. Tonight she was extremely tired. She had been up all night. It was nearly four in the morning.

David insisted again that she go home. No, no, she would stay. She put her head on his shoulder, nearly dozing once or twice. He rubbed the back of her neck and her shoulders. Her back ached; her head ached. He rubbed her forehead and then went somewhere to find her some aspirin. When he came back, he sat and prayed with her, talking to her with tender, soothing words. In her purse she had a New Testament with Psalms, and he took it and read to her.

While he read, she thought a lot about death. Christ had died; her beloved Christ. She thought of that. The Lord Himself had died for her, for David, for Brian.

Once while David rubbed her shoulders, she murmured, "What if Brian dies?" She couldn't recall what David said. Did he answer? What did he say? David read from the Psalms. He prayed, talking out loud. His voice was soft, a gentle melody. Rachel listened, nodding, murmuring yes, yes. She loved God; she loved David. Somehow within her grief there was a harmony, a comforting awareness of God's presence. Even now, God was present. Blessed Christ.

Before dawn, around five or five-thirty, Rachel was aware of something new. A feeling within her belly, a jagged, sudden lurching of something solid inside her. An involuntary reflex of actual pain. Rachel gasped and sat up straight.

"What is it?" said David.

"Nothing. The baby's kicking," cried Rachel over the pain.

"Are you sure?"

She held her body still, waiting, listening, aware of the intricate function of all the parts of her body. Everything was working together, a quiet inner pounding, a steady flow of juices through the network of arteries and veins beneath her skin, the harmony of bones and tissue and muscle and blood. But now there was more. Pain—!

She pressed the flat of her hand against her abdomen on the spot that she knew to be the baby's back. She waited, breathless, for his response. Whenever she nudged him, he moved; he always moved. It was like a game, this gentle nudging and his immediate reflex. Bump him; he bumped back. Nudge. There was nothing. She pressed again, harder. She waited. Nothing. Again! Nothing. Her baby was still. Again she pressed, urgently, demanding a response. Only pain, racing into the myriad cells of her body.

Aloud, to David, she said with mushrooming panic, "Something's wrong with the baby. He doesn't move. I can't feel him move. He's dead, David. I think my baby's dead!"

Chapter Twenty-Three

"Put your clothes in this closet," a nurse was saying. Obediently Rachel undressed, put her clothing away and slipped into a coarse hospital gown. She got up into the large, sturdy bed and covered herself with a sheet, waiting for whatever would happen next.

It was peculiar, this feeling, this sensation. It was too much, thought Rachel. It was taking over. The simple fact was that there was a baby inside her struggling to be born. He would not stop until he saw the light of day. He was more real now than she, this baby, his body more real than her own. It was his show. He was in charge now.

This baby had to live. She could not stand it if this baby were not alive. She could not stand to have a dead baby inside her.

Rachel's mind was ponderous, confused. What was going on? People came and went, doing things for her, to her. They all looked busy, these people in their white, impersonal outfits. They were too busy to talk; they did their business without a word.

"The doctor will be here soon to examine you," the same nurse said, buzzing around the room as if she had a great many duties to perform and would get all of them out of the way as efficiently as possible. She slung a contraption around Rachel's arm, tightened it and took her blood pressure. "Just relax, hon, you'll be okay," the nurse said blandly.

Rachel was grateful for this kind word from a busy nurse. It was more than she expected. Somehow it helped to clear her mind, to focus her thoughts upon her immediate situation. She found the courage to ask, "But my baby, my baby isn't due for a month yet. Since I came up here I haven't felt him move—not a kick or anything."

The nurse placed her stethoscope over several areas of Rachel's bulging abdomen, pausing each time to listen, a mild cryptic expression on her face.

"I hear a heartbeat," she said matter-of-factly, and was gone. She returned moments later with pills in a small paper cup. "These will help you relax," she explained. "You're tighter than a drum. Try to get some rest now."

Rachel swallowed the pills and returned the cup to the nurse's waiting hand. Before the nurse could turn on her heel to leave, Rachel managed to ask, "Where is my husband? Will I be able to see him?"

The nurse was at the door by the time she answered. "I imagine he's down the hall in the expectant father's waiting room. When we have you ready, he can come and stay with you. Are you scheduled for the ABC room—the Alternate Birth Center?"

"No, my husband and I—we—" She faltered. What could she say? I couldn't schedule the Lamaze classes because my husband and I have been separated my entire pregnancy? "We didn't prepare for natural childbirth—"

"Then you'll be having a spinal?"

"I don't know. This has all happened so fast." Lifting herself on one elbow, she asked anxiously, "Nurse, I was wondering, have you heard anything about my son...any word?"

The nurse's crisp expression changed subtly, softening perhaps, but Rachel couldn't quite interpret the change. Shaking her head stiffly, the woman said, "No, no, I'm sorry. I don't know anything about your son."

And she was gone.

Later David appeared in the doorway, looking weary and disheveled as he approached her bedside. Rachel pulled herself into a sitting position and let her legs dangle over the side of the bed so that she could face him while they talked. She had the fleeting impression that it had been days since she had last seen him, not merely two hours. There was a small, fretful smile on his lips that turned up the corners of his mouth like hooks, a smile that no doubt mirrored Rachel's own brittle expression.

"How are you?" he asked, caressing her hair.

"All right. I don't feel too bad, considering."

He kissed the top of her head. "You scared me to death. I thought we were going to lose the baby."

Rachel's smile was splintered, inside out. "I thought so, too."

David searched her eyes. "But he's okay?"

Her smile righted itself and softened perceptibly. "The nurse heard his heartbeat. She said so."

David embraced her gently. "That's wonderful."

Rachel glanced down sheepishly at her gown, at

her own swollen body that turned the gown into a pale, humorless balloon. "I look so terrible," she complained self-consciously.

He looked at her and smiled, his eyes crinkling at the corners. "No, you look beautiful. Like a lovely Madonna."

Her cheeks grew warm. "You haven't said that for a long time. Madonna. I thought you forgot."

"No, I'd never forget." He rubbed her knee with an awkward hand; then, as she relaxed, he rubbed the calf of her leg gently, soothingly. "I'm remembering more all the time, Rae. I'm remembering how much I love you."

She grinned foolishly. "I love you, too."

"That makes me very happy, Rachel."

She smiled into his eyes, feeling lighter somehow, almost pleased, as if they had come through some sort of trial. What was it? A process of learning to respond to each other again? It seemed to Rachel like an important moment, but she had no words to make it tangible, so instead, she tucked the corners of her gown around her thighs and said, "This thing doesn't even have a back, David. A backless gown. The latest fashion statement. How about that?"

He squeezed her knee, smiling, his lips closed in a perfect arc. "On you it looks fine, darling. Extraordinary."

Laughing lightly, Rachel patted his hand. He had such strong, sturdy hands. "You do worlds for my confidence, David."

He stepped back, taking both her slim hands in his, and gave her a thorough appraisal. "Do you really feel all right, Rae? Has the doctor been in to see you yet?"

"No, but they called him. The nurse says he'll be here soon." She wound the corner of the sheet around her finger, making a very neat bandage. In the silence of the room she unwound it, pressing the curl out flat. "David," she said after a moment.

"Yes, honey?"

"You haven't said anything about Brian."

His eyes were suddenly grim, his expression distracted. "There's nothing new. I went in to see him, but he looks the same. Still comatose. Still on the respirator."

She persisted, twisting the sheet again into a ragged knot. "But you will tell me as soon as there's any change—even if it's bad. You will tell me, even if I'm in labor, no matter what?"

"I'll tell you as soon as I find out anything, anything at all. I promise."

"Thank you, David. I had to know that."

Feeling a sudden exhaustion sweep over her, Rachel pulled her legs up under the sheets and lay back. "I'm so tired, David." She tried to smile at him, but her mouth felt fuzzy, her tongue thick. "They gave me something so I could relax."

"Why don't you try to sleep, darling?" He pulled a chair over to the bed, dragging it along the floor, so that it made a scraping sound. He sat down heavily and offered her a smile. "I'll sit right here. I'll be right here if you need me."

Rachel slept until noon, when her obstetrician finally came striding into her room.

Dr. Bernard Oberg was a quietly jovial man, tall and limber, with a shock of red hair that made him look a beguiling thirty instead of a settled forty. With a jocular grin he said, "Well, young lady, it appears your little one is in a hurry to greet the world. Let's take a look and see just how eager he is."

While the physician performed his examination, David stepped out for a breath of fresh air and a quick cup of coffee from the vending machine, returning only after the doctor had completed his examination.

"How's my wife doing?" Rachel heard David ask when the two men met outside her door.

"She's doing fine, Mr. Webber, just fine."

"And the baby?"

"The baby's taking his own sweet time, so she has a while to wait yet. Since the baby's premature, the muscles are tight, so it's going to take a little work on Rachel's part."

Rachel heard the anxiety and exhaustion in David's voice. "Will the baby be all right, being premature and all?"

Dr. Oberg's tone was reassuring. "I really don't see why not. I'd guess the baby is over five pounds. I don't anticipate any problems. As an extra precaution we'll be attaching a fetal monitor. Just to be sure the baby maintains a good, steady heartbeat."

"Good." David sighed. "My wife hasn't had much rest, Doctor. Did you hear about our son?"

"Yes, I heard. I'm sorry."

"Rachel was up all night. I tried to get her to go home, but you know how it is. I just want this delivery to be as easy for her as possible."

"I understand, Mr. Webber. Does Intensive Care know where you are?"

"Yes, I told them," David replied. "And now I'd better get back inside and see how Rachel's doing."

"Well, I have a feeling she's a trouper, Mr. Webber. A strong, brave woman you can be proud of."

"I am proud of her," Rachel heard David say with breaking emotion. "You have no idea, Doctor, how proud I am."

Rachel was sitting up in bed eating lunch when David entered the labor room again. The nurse had already started an IV and had hooked up the fetal monitor. The whooshing *glubbity-glub* of the baby's heartbeat sounded in the room, a steady, consoling rhythm. "I have music to eat by," Rachel told him. "Isn't it amazing? We can hear our baby now. It makes him seem more real."

"What a beautiful sound," said David softly.

They exchanged warm, lingering smiles. She saw love in his eyes and it gave her renewed hope and joy.

"What's this? Breakfast in bed?" he teased gently.

"Lunch. But it's terrible. Look. Clear tea, beef bouillon, plain strawberry gelatin. I could eat a thick steak smothered in mushrooms."

He winked at her. "Leave the steak to me. The nurse said they don't want you to have any food in your stomach."

"I know. But just a little saltine cracker?"

"Sorry, baby. How are the contractions?"

Her hands moved to her distended middle. "Not too bad. They hurt, but I can handle it. But I'm getting impatient now. I want things to hurry up, so I can get back to Brian."

David sat down in the pine chair by her bed and stretched out his long legs. "Listen, Rae, you concentrate on the baby and I'll keep an eye on Brian, okay?" He paused. "By the way, I saw Dr. Oberg out in the hall."

She nodded. "Yes, I heard you. He told me I'm

dilated to three, but the baby won't be born until I'm at ten."

David looked puzzled. "Do you understand that?"

"I understand I have seven to go, and that's too much. I want to get this over with."

"Try to be patient, hon."

Rachel sipped her tea. It was too hot. She poured some water into it from the glass on her bed stand. "I'll try, David," she answered halfheartedly. She ate her wobbly, melting gelatin but had no appetite for the bouillon. Pushing away her tray, she said, "I was going to be all ready for this, David. I have all these books at home on natural childbirth. I even started taking a Lamaze class."

"Don't worry, you'll do fine, darling. Fine."

"But I want to be ready," she insisted. "This is too soon. I don't know if I can do it. I'm so tired—I don't even want to think about it, David. I just want it over."

He reached for her hand and kissed it, one finger at a time. "Soon, darling, soon."

Throughout the afternoon David went back and forth between the maternity ward and the intensive care unit, sitting first with Rachel and then with Brian. Rachel's contractions increased in frequency and intensity. Finally the pain was something she could no longer shrug off or ignore. Her body hardened against the pervasive waves, fighting them. Trying to relax, trying to think of other things, Rachel stared at the ceiling and rubbed against the hardness of her abdomen with her fingertips. Her thoughts kept coming back to this, her baby, the imminence of his birth. There was no turning back. She had to ride this one all the way. It would get worse before it got better.

"You're not relaxing," accused David softly, rubbing her arm.

"What?"

"You're stiff. You're fighting it."

"It hurts."

"I know enough to know you should relax. Try to relax, baby. Let your arms—your body—go limp. Don't fight it."

"I'm trying," she whispered huskily. She looked up into his face. Even without sleep and his hair mussed, he was the most handsome man she had ever seen. "I wish you could stay with me all the way, David."

"You mean, be with you in the delivery room?"

She nodded. "Would you want to?"

His brow furrowed. "I never thought about it. I wasn't there with Brian."

"It wasn't as common then to have fathers in the delivery room. But these days..."

He clasped her hand, interlacing her fingers with his. "Do you want me there, Rae?"

She blinked back tears. "I don't want to be alone."

"Then I'll ask Dr. Oberg."

"You really want to be there?"

"It's my baby, too. His first glimpse should be of his mommy and his daddy."

She pressed his solid hand against her moist cheek. "Thank you, David."

Late in the afternoon Dr. Oberg came again to check Rachel and informed her in his soft, cheerful voice that it would be soon now. She was dilated to seven, he said. Almost at transition. Another hour perhaps, or maybe longer. "Do you want some medication for the discomfort?"

She shook her head vigorously. "No, Doctor. It's better for the baby if I don't have a lot of stuff to dope me up, isn't that right? Didn't I read that somewhere?"

"That's generally true, Rachel," he answered in a noncommittal voice. "But if a little medication can take the edge off the pain and give the mother more strength for the big moment, that can be good for the baby, too."

"But what about a premature baby?" persisted Rachel. "Isn't it better to avoid painkillers?"

"I suppose. But, like I said, it's important for you to be comfortable, too, to save your strength and energy."

Rachel white-knuckled her coarse sheet. "I don't want anything, Dr. Oberg. No anesthetic, please. Nothing."

He patted her arm soothingly, as if she were a temperamental child he wished to appease without actually giving in to her demands. "We'll see when the time comes," he said mildly. "Then if you want a regional anesthetic, a spinal block, fine. If not, and you seem to be doing all right, then perhaps we'll just give you a local anesthetic for the episiotomy."

Rachel flashed him a hopeful smile. "I just want to do everything I can for my baby."

"Of course you do," Dr. Oberg replied cheerfully, turning to go.

David stopped him and said tentatively, "Dr. Oberg, Rachel and I were wondering if I could—if you'd give permission for me to be in the delivery room with her. I know we haven't taken all those fancy classes, but..."

Dr. Oberg smiled warmly. "I think that can be arranged, Mr. Webber. You'll need to wash up and wear surgical scrubs, right down to your shoes. A nurse can help you when the time comes."

"Thank you, Doctor," said Rachel, her gaze meeting David's.

He was beaming, but there was also a hint of terror in his eyes. "Now I'm nervous," he confessed.

Dr. Oberg patted his arm reassuringly. "Don't worry, Mr. Webber, we've never lost a father yet. Seen a few keel over, of course, but we can handle that."

"Thanks," said David with a grudging smile. "I'll do my best to stay on my feet."

"You have the easy part, David," said Rachel. "For you this is a spectator sport. For me it's the main event."

He leaned over and kissed her forehead. "And I'll be right there in your corner cheering you on, darling."

Rachel stiffened and clasped her stomach. "It's going to take more than cheer, David," she cried breathlessly. "I'm having another contraction, and it's bad!"

During the next few hours, to forget the pain, Rachel forced her mind to go over all the events in her life since she'd found out she was pregnant. It was like going over ancient photographs in an old family album. The events were etched in her brain, blending together, sometimes fuzzy, unfocused, with swirling blacks and whites or soft, blurring colors, strung out in her thoughts, obliterating the cramps, the pain.

Photographs. Make them work. Make them happen. One by one. Brian. David. David moving out of the house because he was involved with a girl named Kit.

David's face, the agony, the hurt when he left. Brian's face, the disappointment. Better to recall these memories than to think of the pain now; better, better. Fragments of memory. A possible divorce. Problems with Brian.

It all seemed unreal now, as if her life had happened to someone else, someone Rachel hardly knew, a stranger. Now all of these things were part of the past. As the pain increased, Rachel could no longer summon the images clearly. All the events of her life were stuck somewhere in her brain like bits of shrapnel, out of sight. Nothing surfaced, nothing was clear, but everything was there, hidden, stabbing her consciousness, unrelenting.

Cramps. Waves and waves of cramps knocked her down. If only she could ride with them, stay on top. She was always washed under, left gasping for breath, and befuddled by a wilderness of pain. It didn't matter now that David was there, trying to help, trying to offer comfort. He seemed beyond her, out of reach, his voice distant and remote, his touch more an irritant than encouragement. Leave me alone, she wanted to cry. You can't help me; no one can help me now.

It seemed to Rachel that she was being swallowed up. Spiritually, mentally, physically, she was being consumed. Something more than the baby attacked her, bombarding her will. Her strength was draining away, gone. Her body was a broken dam, ready to spill out its contents and leave her with nothing, empty. Her mind was used up and flying into the wind like confetti.

Where was everything going to end? When? Or had it ended already? Was this the final breaking apart, the ultimate destruction of Rachel Webber?

Chapter Twenty-Four

"You're doing fine, Rae." This a voice miles away, an unreal voice, dreamy.

"David?"

"I'm right here, baby."

"It's getting bad, really bad. I can't do this."

"Should I call the nurse? She could get you something."

"No, I don't want anything. I wish I could remember those breathing techniques. Breathing is important. I don't think I'm breathing right."

"Just relax, baby." David smoothed back her hair, stroking gently. "That's it, relax."

Rachel licked her dry, chapped lips. "I—I'm thirsty."

"I'm sorry, hon. You can't have anything to drink. Doctor's orders. But the nurse left some ice chips."

"Yes. Anything!"

David placed a gleaming sliver of ice between her lips. She welcomed the biting coldness. "More."

David fed her several more chips. "You're doing great, sweetheart. Just hang in there."

"Why don't we hear something about Brian?" she asked plaintively, irritation stealing into her voice. "Why don't they tell us something?"

"The doctor knows where we are," David replied softly. "He said he'd let us know if there's any change at all."

She reached out for David's hand and hugged it against her breast. "David, if Brian dies, I don't want to live, either."

He bent close, his breath warm on her face. "You don't mean that, Rachel."

"I can't imagine living without Brian. How could things ever be the same?"

"They couldn't," he conceded. He moved his mouth gently over her cheek, his lips soft and sweet, his voice tender with yearning. "Rachel, darling, listen to me. This is the time for us to trust the Lord. Not with words, but with our hearts. If we don't trust Him now, we may never trust Him again with anything. This is the test of what we are, what we have, what we believe. Listen, Rae, we have hope. The hope of Christ! Hold on to that."

Rachel's breath was short, hardly there. She murmured, "We have this hope as an anchor for our soul, firm and secure."

"Is that from the Bible?"

"Yes. Somewhere. I believe it, David. Hold on to the hope of Christ."

David caressed her head, her hair. "That's it. Cling to it, Rachel. Hope. It keeps everything else in perspective."

"I'm trying, David." She stiffened suddenly, wrenching away from his caress.

"Rachel, what is it?"

"I feel different. Something's happening, David. I have to push. I can't control it."

"I'll get someone!"

One nurse appeared, then another, scurrying into the room, checking the monitor, examining her, listening with their stethoscopes, bustling about, twittering like quick, earnest birds.

David was quickly waved out of the room. "Follow me, Mr. Webber. We'll get you into your scrubs."

Rachel heard one nurse, a heavy, rawboned woman, exclaim loudly, "Where's Dr. Oberg? This baby's coming!"

"We paged him," someone said. "He's on his way up from the cafeteria."

A moment later Dr. Oberg sauntered in with a confident smile and patted her hand. "We planned this one pretty well, Rachel. I just finished my coffee. How do you feel?"

"I have to push," she cried, panting, breathless. "I can't control it."

"Do you remember feeling that way when your son was born?"

"It was so long ago. I think so, yes."

"You're in the final stage of labor, Rachel. Your baby will be born shortly."

"Hurry!"

"You're doing fine, Rachel," he said. "We're taking you to the delivery room now."

"There's no time, no time!"

"Let me worry about that, Rachel. Did you have the anesthetic?"

"No. I didn't want one. Just hurry, Doctor. Please!"

There was a blur of activity around Rachel. Nothing was clear or well-defined, except for the upheaval within her own body. It was a thing beyond her, gripping her, a stampede of her insides, as if a ton of pressure pummeled the flimsy walls of her flesh, plummeting, plunging. She was caught in the avalanche, losing control.

She was aware of movement, of two attendants rolling her bed into the hallway and down the hall. Just before her gurney was pushed through the open doors into the delivery room, she caught a glimpse of David approaching in a green scrub gown, a surgical cap on his head. "I'm here, Rachel," he called to her. "We're doing this together."

She reached out for him, but the two attendants were already rolling her onto another bed, a hard, slablike table. A nurse covered her trembling legs with sheets and placed her feet in metal stirrups.

Dr. Oberg was saying something about not pushing yet. What? Was he kidding? It was beyond her control. Above her head was a huge, pale light like some sort of moon, out of focus, imaginary. A disc, wide and pervasive, was spraying soft light over the room.

She heard a rustling sound by her head. David was there, sitting down beside her, bending his face to hers, his hands moving to her shoulders, her hair. He massaged the knots of tension in her shoulders, his deft fingers kneading her skin through the coarse hospital gown. "You're doing great," he whispered. "It won't be long now."

Dr. Oberg and the nurses were busy, apparently

unconcerned with her, doing things, obviously synchronized and working together expertly like the mechanical parts of a clock. Perfect precision. Their movements like rhythm, a delicate syncopation.

But Rachel couldn't appreciate their expertise now. "David," she groaned. She was bearing down with what was surely cataclysmic force. Did she have such power, such strength? She was turning herself inside out.

"Not yet, Rachel, not yet." The doctor's voice. He pointed to a mirror overhead in case she cared to watch. She looked away.

Her legs were trembling so hard she couldn't hold them still. A frigid chill had seized her body, and her teeth chattered. Her hands felt clammy and numb as stones.

"Doctor, I—I can't..."

"Hang in there, sweetheart," David urged, smoothing back the damp tendrils of her hair. "You're doing great."

How could he say that? She was going down for the count. How could her baby live when she herself couldn't possibly survive?

Dr. Oberg's voice sounded faint, far away. "All right, Rachel, on the next contraction, I want you to bear down...all right, now. Now, Rachel!"

The waves of the sea slammed against rock, breaking it....

"That's good, Rachel, good. You're doing fine. We have his head. See in the mirror, Rachel? Next his shoulders. A slight turn. Relax a moment. Now take a deep breath. Yes. All right, on the next contraction, another good push. Okay, here it comes. Now push, Rachel, push."

Push, push, push!

Rachel heard a cry. Not her own voice, not her own agonized sigh. No. Her baby.

"A girl, Rachel, a girl!" cried Dr. Oberg, holding the wobbly infant up in the palms of his hands.

"A daughter, Rae!" David gently lifted Rachel up onto her elbows so she could see the smooth, lithe, cheesy body of her daughter. The thick, purplish umbilical cord was still attached, a remnant of their oneness.

"She looks fine, just fine," Dr. Oberg assured them with a light, easy laugh. "Ten fingers, ten toes, everything in place."

David leaned over and kissed Rachel soundly on the mouth, his breath minty, his warm skin smelling faintly of lime. Tears glistened in his eyes. "You were wonderful, Rae. I've never loved you more than I do this moment."

Rachel lifted her hand gingerly and touched David's face, moving her fingers over his stubbled cheek, his sturdy chin. The icy trembling in her limbs was gone. A delicious, satisfying warmth washed over her. She whispered, "I love you, too."

The nurses were already working with the child, cleaning mucus from her nose and mouth. Rachel couldn't see all they did, but she heard the steady cry, the lovely, healthy cry of her baby. Within minutes a nurse wheeled a small bassinet over beside her so she and David could watch their daughter while the doctor finished his work.

Rachel couldn't take her eyes off the small, thrashing, squealing infant at her side. Her darling child had fine, downy black hair, a red face and white, clenched fists as delicate and translucent as pearls. Her tiny feet kicked the air and her miniature belly heaved with sobs. "Isn't she gorgeous, David?"

"Nearly as beautiful as her mother."

"Wait till Brian sees his little sister. If anything can make him want to get well..."

"Would you like to put your daughter to the breast?" asked the nurse.

Rachel hesitated. "Now? Already? I don't know..."

"Go on," David urged. "She sounds plenty hungry to me."

"Rachel's face grew pleasantly warm. "I—I'll try."

The nurse rested the squirming infant on Rachel's chest and helped the rooting baby connect with her source of nourishment. "She won't get much yet, but it's good practice for both of you," the nurse said with an approving smile.

As their daughter nursed, David nestled his chin against the top of Rachel's head and gently stroked the baby's downy, fine angel hair. As she watched her eager, ravenous child suckle and savored David's encircling warmth, Rachel felt a tender bond knitting the three of them to one another, a tie as strong as the cords of forgiveness, as thick as the blood in their veins, as eternal as heaven itself. She tucked the magical moment into her memory like a cherished treasure to savor during the painful, unpredictable days ahead.

Chapter Twenty-Five

The next morning Rachel awoke in her hospital room. The drapes were pulled back and sunlight streamed in, turning the walls a warm, creamy yellow. Blinking against the brightness, Rachel pulled her tangled thoughts from the grogginess of slumber. She still had that warm, fuzzy feeling about her that comes from sound sleep. She could not quite distinguish the warm, languorous sections of her body from the cocoon warmth of blankets and sheets. She stretched, testing the separate parts of her body for pain and discomfort. Not too bad. No, not bad at all.

Her body was empty. She had delivered a beautiful, healthy baby girl, and it was a warm, delicious feeling. She praised God, the giver of life. Wonderful life.

Within Rachel was a perfect silence, a hush, although she could hear the muted hospital sounds outside her room. Voices. Distant, insistent baby cries from the nursery down the hall. Carts wheeling about. The metallic *clickety-clack* of utensils and trays. Padded, purposeful footsteps. Sounds fading in and out, the constant, quiet hum of hospital noise. But within Rachel was a simple quiet. Peace.

She was ready for this day—Sunday, yes, Sunday. She was ready for whatever would come. For whatever news David would bring of their son. Ready. God was making even the ache of worry over Brian somehow bearable. A wellspring of peace inside her smoothed out the jaggedness of anxiety and fear.

She recalled familiar words that spoke of God's comfort. "You will keep him in perfect peace, whose mind is stayed on You, because he trusts in You." Yes! No longer just words, but reality. Something to live by and hold on to, no matter what came. It was clear to her now: Jesus Christ was her reality. She owed Him her life, all that she was, all she ever would be. It was a blessed, wonderful obligation, one which David also shared, willingly, gladly. Together, no matter what happened, they would be all right; they would make it. Their priorities were in order.

And Brian, their son. Still a question mark. *Oh, God, let Brian live,* thought Rachel prayerfully. *Let him be healthy and whole.*

David showed up a few minutes after Rachel's breakfast tray had been removed. He still had the walk of a weary man, but his face was shaven and there was a special light in his eyes that Rachel recognized as his love for her. A lovely, welcome light, his love.

Rachel sat up in bed. "David, Brian—what about Brian? Have you seen him?

"Yes, I just came from his room." He gave her a quick kiss on the lips, then took both her hands in his. "He's better, Rachel. He started breathing on his own early this morning,'' said David, rubbing his large hands over her vulnerable, small ones.

''Breathing? Then...then he's all right? He'll be all right?''

David pulled her close to him and kissed her forehead and hair. ''Darling, Brian's starting to come out of the coma. The doctor says he's past the crisis. He's not out of the woods yet. He has a long way to go, and we have a long way to go with him, but yes, I think he will be all right. I really do think he'll pull through.''

''Thank God, David.''

''It could so easily have gone the other way. Brian could have died. This morning I sat by his bed holding his hand, just watching him. I suppose it was silly, but I even talked to him. I kept praying he could hear me. I told him about the baby and said we were all going to be a family again. I even mentioned that we might move to Cleveland, where he could see his grandparents and have a house with a big yard. But I said it's definitely up to his mom, because I won't go anywhere without her.''

''A house and a yard, you said?''

''Sure, why not?'' said David. ''With the new baby we've outgrown the condo. And haven't you always wanted a roomy house of our own and a big yard where our children could play? Maybe one of those old Victorians you love or even a farmhouse. A place in the country with a garden and a picket fence and maybe even some dogs and cats and who knows what else?''

Rachel hugged her husband. ''David, you know how I've always wanted a home like that. It would be wonderful!''

"We'll have that and more. We'll have a Christian home, darling."

Rachel studied her husband's face, trying to read his expression. "David, we are going to be all right, aren't we...all four of us?"

He gently massaged her shoulder. "I hope so, darling. Of course, there will be things to deal with. Some sort of therapy or counseling for Brian, for the three of us. Showing him we're a family again, that we want to be a Christ-centered family. It won't be easy, Rachel. Brian may recover physically—I pray that he does. But how will he be emotionally and spiritually? We can't predict what scars he may have. We have to be ready to do everything possible to win Brian back. But with the Lord's help, we can do it.

"I telephoned Marlene and Pastor Emrick and filled them in on what's happened," David continued, "and they're both praying. And I have a surprise for you. Marlene is here to see you."

"Marlene? Here?"

"Her friend Mr. Timmons drove her over."

Rachel looked around. "Where is she? Why didn't she come in?"

"She stopped by the nursery to see the baby. But I think she wanted to give us a little time alone. She'll be right in."

"If I'm having visitors I'd better look presentable." Rachel reached for her pink satin robe at the foot of the bed and swung it around her shoulders. "Thanks for bringing in my things."

"Oh, the nurse gave you the suitcase I brought in?"

"Yes, first thing this morning," said Rachel, her fingers busy with the soft, quilted buttons of the robe.

"Good. I thought you'd like having your own stuff...nightgowns, a bathrobe, your toothbrush."

"Yes, my negligees sure are better than those sleazy hospital gowns."

"They sure are, darling." David winked. "There's no comparison." He looked around. "Did I remember everything?"

"Yes, David. Thank you. You're—"

A light rapping on the door was followed by a familiar cheery voice. "Anybody home?"

"Come in, Marlene," called Rachel.

Marlene slipped in the door and gave Rachel a questioning smile. "Hi, sweetie. How's the new mommy? Are you up for company?" She was wearing a touch of makeup and the black chemise she had purchased on their recent shopping trip. Rachel had never seen her look prettier.

"You're not company," Rachel told her, returning the smile. "You're family."

David pulled a chair over beside Rachel's bed. "Sit here, Marlene."

She went first to Rachel and kissed her cheek. "You have the most beautiful little baby girl in that nursery! I mean, all the little boy babies were winking at her and flirting up a storm. You're going to have to watch that one. You'll have to be chasing off the boys with a baseball bat before she's five."

"She is beautiful, isn't she?" said Rachel, pleased.

Marlene took the chair David offered and gazed back at Rachel. "And look at you, girl! You look gorgeous. If I could look that good after having a baby, I'd consider getting pregnant, too. Of course, I'd have to hog-tie myself a man first."

"From what I understand, Mr. Timmons is an excellent candidate," said Rachel slyly.

Marlene's cheeks reddened. "He just might fill the bill. And the best part is—he likes me!"

Rachel smiled. "I don't know anybody who can resist you, Marlene."

"Ditto," said David. "You just go out there and charm the socks off that man."

Marlene rolled her eyes. "Oh, you two are going to make me blush!" They all laughed. Then, after a moment, Marlene's tone grew serious. She made a sad face and rubbed her arm distractedly. "I owe you both a huge apology."

"What for?" asked Rachel, puzzled.

"Why, baby, for not taking care of Brian. I can't tell you how guilty I feel. I went by the ICU and peeked in on Brian. He's got to be okay."

"There's nothing for you to feel guilty about, Marlene," David assured her. "Brian's the one who snuck away. He's the one who chose to disobey."

Marlene pulled a tissue from her purse and blew her nose. "But somehow I should have been able to protect him."

"We feel that way as parents, too, Marlene," Rachel admitted. "It's always easier to look back and see what you should have done."

David nodded. "We all trusted the boy, and it backfired."

"But you left me in charge," said Marlene, dabbing her eyes. "Brian came over and we had a nice dinner—fried chicken and chocolate pie, his favorites. I walked him home, and when I dropped in an hour or so later he was sitting at his desk with his books spread around. He assured me he was studying."

David's brow furrowed. "I'm sure Brian planned all along to sneak out. He was just waiting for his chance."

"He told me I didn't have to check on him again because he was tired and going to bed early. But I was going to anyway before I went to bed. Then Mr. Timmons—Stanley—called. We got to talking and the time just flew. It was too late to go back over and check on Brian. I glanced out at your place through my kitchen window and saw all the lights off. I didn't want to wake him." Marlene's voice broke. "I never dreamed in a million years he'd sneak out like that."

"None of us imagined he'd do something like that," said David, "or we never would have left him alone."

"He will be all right, won't he? What do the doctors say?"

"The news is good," said David. "Brian's off the respirator. He's coming out of the coma."

Rachel sat up and threw back her blanket. "And now it's time for me to get out of bed and go see my children. I want to check out those little boy babies who've been ogling our daughter." Her voice caught with emotion. "And then I want to go see Brian and sit by his bed, so I'll be the first one he sees when he wakes up."

"Are you sure you're up to all that?" asked David.

"Positive. I've got to see my son…and my new little daughter." A light broke in Rachel's eyes, as if something important had suddenly dawned on her, and she exclaimed, "David, do you realize…?"

He looked up, startled. "What?"

"Can you believe it? We haven't even thought of a name for her yet."

"Well, that's extremely important," said Marlene. "You can't call her Miss X for the rest of her life. She has to have a name."

David nodded. "A name. Something she can live with."

"Do you have any ideas, Marlene?" asked Rachel.

Marlene put her finger to her cheek, a sly smile curling her lips. "Let me think. My family is marvelous at coming up with names. I know lots of names. I have scads of relatives with names."

"Oh, Marlene, you're a riot."

With a whimsical smile, Marlene pursed her lips and tapped her finger against her chin. "There's my aunt, Eugenia Weatherspoon. And her daughter Delphinium. And my cousin Lucretia Quailbush. And her sister, Ernestine. And, of course, my grandmother, the matriarch of them all, Henrietta Lingerfelter."

Rachel's eyes narrowed slyly. "Marlene, you're making up those names, aren't you!"

Marlene smiled triumphantly. "You'll never know!"

David's voice took on a slightly mocking tone. "Well, Marlene, obviously we wouldn't want to encroach on your family's creative genius by borrowing any of those fine names."

"Oh, be my guest! We have lots more!"

"Thanks...but no, thanks."

"Wait, I have one, David!"

"You do, Rachel? Quick! What is it?"

"Hope."

"Hope?" he echoed thoughtfully. "Miss Hope Webber. Hope. Yes, you know, I like it. That's good."

"It's certainly an appropriate name."

"Yes, it is. And it beats Lucretia by at least a mile."

Rachel touched David's arm lightly with her fingertips. "I want to go see her, David. Let's go down to the nursery together right now and see Miss Hope Webber and tell her she has a loving family waiting for her, waiting to take her home."

David helped Rachel out of bed and supported her with his arms until she was able to stand on her feet. "Rae," he said, his tone concerned, protective, "are you sure it won't be too long a walk for you?"

"Oh, no," she cried. "It will be a wonderful walk. But I need you beside me. And you, too, Marlene, on the other side. I'm still a little clumsy on my feet. See? I have to lean on you both."

Rachel put her arm around David and leaned happily against him while Marlene took her other arm. "Okay, I'm ready," Rachel said, smiling.

After a few steps Marlene released Rachel's arm and stepped away. "I don't think you two need me," she said gently. "I think you can make it on your own just fine."

"Lady, I think you're right." David gave Marlene an approving wink, then turned back to his wife. "How about it, darling? Are you sure you're ready for this?"

She smiled through sudden tears. "With you beside me, David, I'm ready for anything."

"I'll hold you to that, Rae. I'm never leaving your side." Impulsively he bent his head and kissed Rachel full on the lips, a slow, simmering, magnificent kiss. Then, while her heart lingered in a dreamy haze, he circled her waist with his arm and led her out of the room and down the hall to the nursery…where Hope was waiting.

Epilogue

Sunday, April 25

Dear Marlene,

I was so excited to receive your wonderful invitation to be the matron of honor at your wedding in June. You sounded so happy in your letter. I know you've dreamed of this day for a long time. Stanley Timmons is a very lucky man, and it means so much that you want me to be a member of your wedding party. I accept...gladly!

I will be bringing David, Brian and Hope with me. We've decided to make it a special vacation. Brian wants to see some of his old friends, including Ronnie Mayhew, who just got out of a teen halfway house and seems to be trying to put his life back together.

And of course, Brian insists that we do every theme park in the state! And while

Hope may be too young to try the amusement rides, I know she'd love a petting zoo.

You should see all the animals we have here on our farm. Not just cats and dogs, but goats and chickens, rabbits and sheep. Brian joined the 4-H club and he's raising his own heifer. He says someday Bessie could end up on our dinner table, but I told him I won't eat anything that can look me in the eye.

But we all love the farm, even David. It's a bit of a commute for him, but he works at home on his own computer several days a week. With him here to help care for the kids, I've had time to finish my counseling degree. I'm working with another drama group with our church here, and I love it. We've done programs for several teen centers and women's shelters, and when my kids are older I may even become a full-time counselor.

Would you believe? I spend a lot of time in my garden. I'm trying my hand at growing vegetables—tomatoes, green beans, peas and sweet corn. My crops have been a little skimpy so far, but David assures me I'll get the hang of it eventually.

David built a little gazebo in our backyard, and on summer nights we sit out under the stars and sip apple cider and listen to our favorite CDs like lovesick teenagers. David's parents love having the kids over on weekends, so David and I often have the house to ourselves.

We take long walks down by the creek and let the crickets serenade us, or we curl up in front of the TV with my Persian cat and David's mongrel dog—part collie, part German shepherd and a dozen other varieties thrown in.

We've managed to find a simpler, more leisurely life-style here on the farm. It's been good for our marriage and good for our family.

Brian's settled down, and at fifteen he seems content and his grades are good. And, of course, he adores his little sister. If anybody ever messes with her, they've got Brian to answer to. She's still a bouncy, energetic toddler who loves to chase the baby chicks, and she's devoted to her older brother.

I've included a few photographs, Marlene, so you can see how the kids have grown. And in two short months we'll be there in person to celebrate your wedding and catch up on all the news.

Thanks for always being there for me, Marlene. You've been a wonderful friend. And thank you for introducing our family to the Lord Jesus, our very best Friend of all!

With lots of love,
Rachel

* * * * *

Dear Reader,

We women love a great romance, don't we? Not only do we love to read about them in the pages of romance novels, but we hope to live that great romance in our own marriage, as well. Unfortunately, reality rarely measures up to fantasy, because marriage is, after all, the union of two flawed, needy human beings who expect to find their deepest needs met in their mate.

The best marriages I've seen are those in which both husband and wife have, first of all, a personal and fulfilling relationship with God. Their needs are met daily by God's abundant, unconditional love, so that when they come together as husband and wife, they respond not out of their own neediness but rather, with an overflow of God's love. They focus on giving rather than taking.

I know from thirty-one years of marriage that I feel much more loving and giving toward my husband, Bill, when I have first spent time alone with God, experiencing God's love and forgiveness and healing Spirit. When I place my expectations on Christ rather than on my husband, we're both happier! A consistent, fulfilling spiritual life is the best recipe I know for a healthy, satisfying marriage.

In *Rachel's Hope*, I gave David and Rachel's marriage a plethora of problems. I wanted to show the crises that resulted when David and Rachel tried to fill the void in their lives in ways that left God out. Only when they turned to the One who made them and knew and loved them best could they begin to put the pieces of their lives and their marriage together.

Dear reader, I hope you and the one you love have discovered how deeply and abundantly God loves you, just as you are at this very moment in time. There's nothing we can do to earn His love. He just wants us to open our hearts and accept Him. I invite you to step out by faith, rest upon Him and soar joyously on the wings of His love. Believe me, that's the ultimate romance!

Warmly,

Carole Gift Page

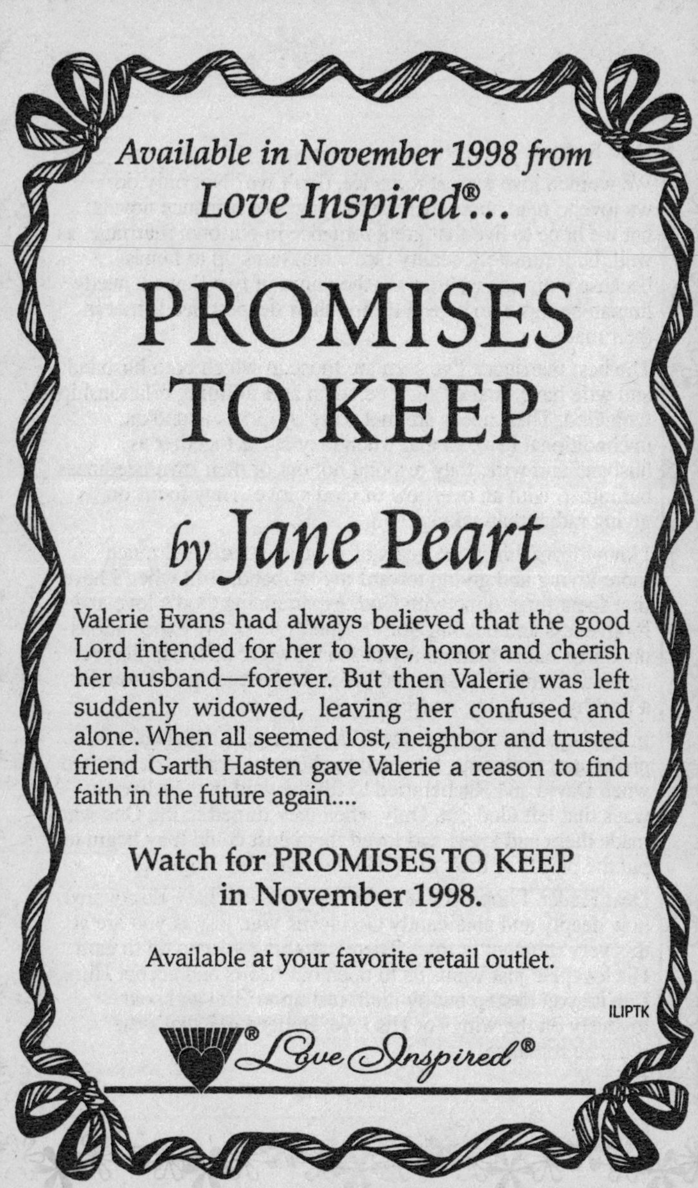
Available in November 1998 from
Love Inspired®...
PROMISES
TO KEEP
by Jane Peart
Valerie Evans had always believed that the good Lord intended for her to love, honor and cherish her husband—forever. But then Valerie was left suddenly widowed, leaving her confused and alone. When all seemed lost, neighbor and trusted friend Garth Hasten gave Valerie a reason to find faith in the future again....
Watch for PROMISES TO KEEP
in November 1998.
Available at your favorite retail outlet.
ILIPTK
Love Inspired®

Take 3 inspirational love stories FREE!
PLUS get a FREE surprise gift!
Special Limited-time Offer
Mail to Steeple Hill Reader Service™
3010 Walden Avenue
P.O. Box 1867
Buffalo, N.Y. 14240-1867
YES! Please send me 3 free Love Inspired™ novels and my free surprise gift. Then send me 3 brand-new novels every month, which I will receive months before they appear in bookstores. Bill me at the low price of $3.19 each plus 25¢ delivery and applicable sales tax, if any*. That's the complete price and a saving of over 10% off the cover prices—quite a bargain! I understand that accepting the books and gift places me under no obligation ever to buy any books. I can always return a shipment and cancel at any time. Even if I never buy another book from Steeple Hill, the 3 free books and the surprise gift are mine to keep forever.
103 IEN CFAG
Name (PLEASE PRINT)
Address Apt. No.
City State Zip
This offer is limited to one order per household and not valid to present Love Inspired™ subscribers. *Terms and prices are subject to change without notice. Sales tax applicable in New York.
ULI-198
©1997 Steeple Hill

Available in November 1998 from
Love Inspired®...
TWO RINGS, ONE HEART
by Martha Mason
Mitch Whitney returned to his family looking for forgiveness. Finally he felt emotionally ready to take on his responsibilities as father and husband. However, would his family be ready to accept him back into their lives? A woman of strong faith, Megan had never stopped loving Mitch, but could she learn to trust him again?
Available at your favorite retail outlet.
Love Inspired®
ILI2R

Available in
October 1998 from
Love Inspired®
A FATHER'S
PROMISE
by Marta Perry
It was an answer to a prayer when Leigh Christopher bonded with Daniel Gregory's deaf daughter. Finally, she could use her gift for teaching—until her plans to encourage young Sarah to gain more independence were derailed by her promising pupil's fiercely protective father. Somehow, someway, she vowed to forge a bright new tomorrow with this man and child!
Watch for
A FATHER'S PROMISE
in October 1998
from
Love Inspired®
Available at your
favorite retail outlet.
ILIAFH